The lovemaking t... beyond descriptio...

So beautiful. Pure splendor. Whenever Deedee remembered it, her heart beat with a wild tempo, and a smile formed on her lips. She loved Ryan MacAllister with every breath in her body.

Deedee opened her eyes. Wide.

When, exactly, had she fallen in love with Ryan? She didn't know. But she had a sneaking suspicion she'd broken the rules of their relationship. Crossed the boundaries they'd set.

Friends and lovers. Nothing more.

Oh, yes, Ryan was her friend. Ryan was her lover.

But Ryan was also the man she loved.

Oh, Lord. When she gummed up the program, Deedee thought dryly, she didn't mess around. And now...

Now she was waiting to learn if she was going to have Ryan's baby!

Dear Reader,

Welcome to Silhouette **Special Edition**...welcome to romance. This month we have six wonderful books to celebrate Valentine's Day just right!

Premiering this month is our newest promotion. THAT'S MY BABY! will alternate with THAT SPECIAL WOMAN! and will feature stories from some of your favorite authors. Marking this very special debut is *The Cowboy and His Baby* by Sherryl Woods. It's the third book of her heartwarming series AND BABY MAKES THREE.

Reader favorite Christine Rimmer returns to North Magdalene for another tale of THE JONES GANG in her book, *The Man, The Moon and The Marriage Vow*. The wonderful Joan Elliott Pickart continues her newest series, THE BABY BET, in Special Edition this month. *Friends, Lovers...and Babies!* is book two of the MacAllister family series. Also in February, Pamela Toth introduces the Buchanan Brothers in *Buchanan's Bride*— it's the first book in her series, BUCKLES & BRONCOS. Sharon De Vita's *Child of Midnight* is her first for Special Edition, a passionate story about a runaway boy, a caring woman and the renegade cop who loves them both. And finally, Kelly Jamison's *The Wedding Contract* is a marriage-of-convenience story not to be missed!

So join us for an unforgettable February! I hope you enjoy all these stories!

Sincerely,

Tara Gavin
Senior Editor

Please address questions and book requests to:
Silhouette Reader Service
U.S.: 3010 Walden Ave., P.O. Box 1325, Buffalo, NY 14269
Canadian: P.O. Box 609, Fort Erie, Ont. L2A 5X3

JOAN ELLIOTT PICKART

FRIENDS, LOVERS... AND BABIES!

Published by Silhouette Books

America's Publisher of Contemporary Romance

If you purchased this book without a cover you should be aware
that this book is stolen property. It was reported as "unsold and
destroyed" to the publisher, and neither the author nor the
publisher has received any payment for this "stripped book."

I would like to thank Yavapai County Deputy Sheriff
Deon Robison and Deputy Sheriff Gary Ferrato for
their information regarding police procedures.

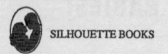 SILHOUETTE BOOKS

ISBN 0-373-24011-2

FRIENDS, LOVERS...AND BABIES!

Copyright © 1996 by Joan Elliott Pickart

All rights reserved. Except for use in any review, the reproduction
or utilization of this work in whole or in part in any form by any
electronic, mechanical or other means, now known or hereafter
invented, including xerography, photocopying and recording, or in
any information storage or retrieval system, is forbidden without
the written permission of the editorial office, Silhouette Books,
300 East 42nd Street, New York, NY 10017 U.S.A.

All characters in this book have no existence outside the imagination of
the author and have no relation whatsoever to anyone bearing the same
name or names. They are not even distantly inspired by any individual
known or unknown to the author, and all incidents are pure invention.

This edition published by arrangement with Harlequin Books S.A.

® and TM are trademarks of Harlequin Books S.A., used under
license. Trademarks indicated with ® are registered in the United States
Patent and Trademark Office, the Canadian Trade Marks Office and in
other countries.

Printed in U.S.A.

Books by Joan Elliott Pickart

Silhouette Special Edition

*Friends, Lovers...
  and Babies! #1011

*The Baby Bet

Silhouette Desire

*Angels and Elves #961

**Previously published under
the pseudonym Robin Elliott**

Sihouette Special Edition

Rancher's Heaven #909
Mother at Heart #968

Silhouette Intimate Moments

Gauntlet Run #206

Silhouette Desire

Call It Love #213
To Have It All #237
Picture of Love #261
Pennies in the Fountain #275
Dawn's Gift #303
Brooke's Chance #323
Betting Man #344
Silver Sands #362
Lost and Found #384
Out of the Cold #440
Sophie's Attic #725
Not Just Another Perfect Wife #818
Haven's Call #859

JOAN ELLIOTT PICKART

is the author of over sixty-five novels. When she isn't
writing, she enjoys watching football, knitting, reading, gardening and attending craft shows on the town
square. Joan has three daughters and a fantastic little
grandson. Her three dogs and one cat allow her to live
with them in a cozy cottage in a charming small town
in the high pine country of Arizona.

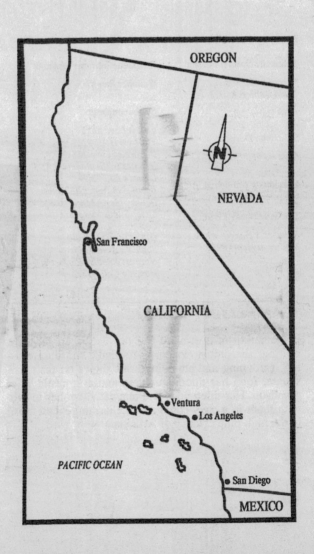

Prologue

A picture-perfect California sunset streaked across the sky as the patrol car moved slowly along the residential street of Ventura. The windows of the vehicle were rolled down, and the officer who was driving inhaled deeply.

"Oh, yeah," he said, glancing over at his partner. "Can you smell that, Ted? Someone is barbecuing."

"Smell it?" Ted Sharpe said. "MacAllister, I'm drooling on my shirtfront. There is nothing finer than food that has been cooked on an outdoor grill."

Ryan MacAllister frowned. "Sherry and I got a barbecue for a wedding present. We've been married seven months, and the thing is still in the box."

"So drag it out, put it together and cook some

steaks. This is June, summer is upon us and barbecuing is part of the package."

"That's not the point," Ryan said. "With our weather a guy could cook outside year-round if he wanted to. What I'm saying is, Sherry and I don't eat many meals together because of our work schedules. Her shift at the hospital and mine on the police force rarely match up. We hardly see each other, unless you want to count watching each other sleep."

"Really? I don't remember you complaining about work schedules before you got married."

"It wasn't a problem then," Ryan said. "She was a floor nurse and her shifts matched mine the majority of the time. She had put in for a transfer to the emergency room, but had been waiting so long for an opening that we really didn't think about it."

"And?"

"And," Ryan said, shaking his head, "the transfer came through a couple of weeks after we were married. Ever since then, we've had one helluva time connecting with each other. I was hoping it would straighten out somehow, but it hasn't. It sure as hell hasn't."

"That's rough," Ted Sharpe said, nodding. "I mean, hell, you're still newlyweds. I imagine you'd want to be together every minute you could."

"No joke. Sherry's on duty now and will get off in about a half an hour. She'll spend the evening alone, then go to bed. I'll get home about two hours before she has to get up and report back to the hospital. It's nuts."

"Have you two talked about it?"

"Sure. Sherry could be a floor nurse again, or go into private care. You know, tend to someone in their house on a straight eight-hour day until their family comes home from work. There are a lot of openings for that kind of nurse. Or she could work in a doctor's office."

"Sounds good."

"Yeah, but Sherry's not having any of it," Ryan said, then sighed wearily. "She waited a long time for that transfer, and she likes the excitement and challenge of the emergency room. She doesn't want to go back on the floor, and said she'd be bored out of her mind in an office or private home. She's an emergency room nurse, and that's that. End of story."

Ryan turned the corner and drove slowly down the next residential street. He raised one finger in greeting to a young boy riding a bike.

"Cute kid," he said. "That's another thing, Ted. I want a family. Sherry and I discussed it before we were married and agreed to wait a couple of years but..." His voice trailed off.

"But?" Ted said.

"You were at the hospital with me when my sister, Andrea, and her husband, John, became parents of twins. You saw Noel and Matt right after they were born. Well, they're four months old already, and they're really something special.

"Every time I see those babies, I realize I don't want to wait to start a family. I'm thirty-five years old, for Pete's sake. I want to have kids while I'm still young enough to enjoy them. You know, go camping, play ball, all kinds of stuff."

Ted chuckled. "You're an old-fashioned dude, MacAllister. Me? I'm very satisfied with the singles scene, thank you very much." He paused and his smile faded. "Ryan, you and Sherry are headed for some heavy-duty problems. I've seen it happen to a lot of cops on shift work. Marriages get blown away. Big time. Don't think it's going to solve itself, because it's not. You'd better tackle it straight on before it's too late."

"Believe me, Ted," Ryan said, nodding, "I've given a lot of thought to exactly what you're saying. Sherry and I are going to have to sit down and—"

Ryan was interrupted by the squawk of the radio, then the voice of the female dispatcher.

"All available units One-Beaver-Three. There is a four-seventeen in the R room at Valley Hospital. Approach code three."

Ryan slammed on the brakes, not hearing the numerous officers responding to the dispatcher's message. The color drained from his face and his hands tightened on the steering wheel until his knuckles turned white.

In the next instant he hit a switch, then pressed hard on the accelerator.

"What are you doing?" Ted said, his eyes widening.

"Code three. Lights and siren," Ryan said, a pulse beating wildly in his temple.

"MacAllister, are you crazy? She said One-Beaver-Three. That's not our sector, not even close. We can't go over there. What in the hell are you doing?"

"Damn it, Ted," he yelled. "There's a shooting in progress in the emergency room at Valley. *Sherry is on duty in that R room!*"

"Lord," Ted said, dragging one hand down his face. He shook his head. "Ryan, we can't leave our sector."

"Go to hell, Sharpe," Ryan said, increasing his speed. "I'm driving. It'll fall on me. You're just along for the ride."

Despite the fact that vehicles pulled quickly to the side of the road as Ryan approached, it seemed to him that everything was moving in agonizingly slow motion. The screaming siren matched the horrifying voice beating against his brain.

Shooting in progress . . . four-seventeen . . . four-seventeen . . . shooting in progress . . . Sherry . . . Sherry . . . Sherry . . .

Ted kept silent, not wanting to do anything to break his partner's concentration as he drove at breakneck speed.

Ryan was going to catch hell for what he was doing, Ted thought, mentally throwing up his hands in defeat. But he would do exactly the same thing. He knew he would. He'd be prepared to pay whatever career consequences came down, just as Ryan was. Hell, MacAllister, drive faster!

Ryan whipped around the corner of the block where Valley Hospital was located, slowed his speed, then hit the brakes as he was blocked by numerous patrol cars with their lights flashing. Two unmarked dark sedans were also there, along with a fire truck. Several vans with television station call letters painted on the sides sat on the fringes.

A group of uniformed police officers kept an ever-growing crowd back from the hospital, and two officers were stringing yellow tape between wooden sawhorses.

Ryan left the patrol car and raced toward the hospital. Before he'd gone twenty feet, a man in a dark suit and tie gripped Ryan's upper arms to halt him. The man staggered slightly from the impact of Ryan plowing into him at full speed.

"MacAllister," the man said, "what in the hell are you doing here?"

Ryan ripped his arms free of the man's hold.

"I'm going in there, Captain," he said, a steely edge to his voice. "Over you, through you, whatever it takes, I'm going in there. My wife, Sherry, is a nurse on duty in that R room."

"Sherry MacAllister," Captain Bolstad said under his breath, then muttered an earthy expletive. He didn't move from in front of Ryan.

"Slow down. Take it easy," the captain said quietly. "It's all over in there. The shooter went berserk, was strung out on drugs. He's dead, Ryan. He turned the weapon on himself after he... Look, let's go to my vehicle where we can have some privacy. This place is crawling with television camera crews."

"Why? Why do you want me to go to your vehicle?" Ryan grabbed the lapels of Captain Bolstad's suit. "Where is Sherry?"

Ted hurried forward and clamped a hand on one of Ryan's biceps.

"Ryan, let him go," Ted said. "Get your hands off of the captain, for God's sake."

Ryan ignored Ted as he tightened his hold on Captain Bolstad's jacket.

"Ryan," the captain said, "Sherry was shot."

"What?" he said, his voice a hoarse whisper. "How bad is it? Where is she? I have to go to her."

"I'll take you to her," Captain Bolstad said, "but...ah, hell, Ryan, I'm sorry. Your wife...Sherry is...Sherry is dead."

Fury and agonizing pain consumed Ryan with such intensity that a red haze blurred his vision. He dropped his hands from the captain's jacket and took a step backward, shaking his head.

"No," he said, "you're lying, you bastard. Sherry is alive. She's my wife and I love her. She wouldn't die and leave me. You're crazy. Tell me where she is, or I'll take you apart."

Captain Bolstad raised both hands. "Okay, Ryan, we'll go inside the hospital. Ted will come with us."

"Come on, buddy," Ted said, his voice strained with emotion. He placed one hand flat on Ryan's back.

"Get away from me," Ryan yelled, then took off at a run toward the hospital.

"Damn," Captain Bolstad said. "Let's go, Ted."

The two men ran after Ryan. The crowd chattered among themselves, speculating as to what was happening. The television crews filmed the drama on the chance there might be a further story unfolding.

Inside the hospital emergency room, the milling police officers, doctors and nurses had become statue still. An eerie silence hung over the area as Captain Bolstad and Ted entered.

Ryan was kneeling on the floor, holding Sherry in his arms, rocking back and forth and whispering her name over and over. The front of Sherry's white uniform was covered in blood, staining Ryan's shirt and pants.

Sherry MacAllister was dead.

Ryan MacAllister wept.

Three days later at ten o'clock in the morning, Sherry was buried beneath a mulberry tree in a nearby cemetery.

At two o'clock that afternoon, Ryan resigned from the police force.

Chapter One

Twenty Months Later

"Happy birthday to you!"

Deedee Hamilton sang the last line of the traditional song at the top of her lungs and terribly off-key.

"Hooray!" she yelled, clapping her hands along with the others who had gathered for the celebration. "You're both officially two years old. Isn't that wonderful?"

The two-year-olds in the limelight did not appear particularly impressed by the festivities. Matt frowned, obviously confused by the adult nonsense he was being subjected to. Noel sucked her thumb and ignored the entire performance.

"We've got a couple of real party animals here," Robert MacAllister, the twins' grandfather, said. "They're so excited, they can hardly hold themselves back."

Andrea, the toddlers' mother, laughed. "They think we're all nuts. Their hats didn't score any points. Let's see if the presents spark some interest. I want to take oodles of pictures of them opening their gifts, then we'll have some cake and ice cream."

A few minutes later, everyone was gathered in the large living room. Once the babies were shown how to tear away the bright wrapping paper, they dove in with enthusiasm, to the delight of their audience.

Deedee sat on the sofa, smiling and laughing along with the others at the antics of the now-happy children. She paused for a moment and glanced around the room.

How fortunate she was, she mused, to have been welcomed into the loving embrace of this wonderful family. They treated her as though she were one of them, including her in all their celebrations throughout the year. The darling twins were being taught to call her Aunt Deedee, a role she did *not* take lightly.

Mentally counting her blessings, she took an inventory of the people attending the babies' birthday party.

Robert and Margaret MacAllister were the senior MacAllisters.

Their oldest son, Michael, and his youngest brother, Forrest, represented MacAllister Architects, Incorporated, a prestigious firm the elder MacAllister had started on a shoestring many years ago. Robert was now retired, and he and Margaret enjoyed their leisure time by traveling, and being devoted grandparents.

Michael was married to Jenny, and had a son, Bobby, who had turned three a few months before. Bobby eyed the gifts wistfully, but seemed to understand that his cousins were the birthday boy and girl.

Andrea, the youngest MacAllister, was married to John, and had her hands full with the busy twins. Her degree in landscape architecture made her an extremely valuable asset to the family firm and she was once again working on a part-time basis, preferring to spend the majority of her day with the babies.

Forrest MacAllister was married to Deedee's dear friend, Jillian Jones-Jenkins, a highly successful author of many historical romance novels.

Deedee smiled as she looked at Jillian.

Jillian had that special, lovely glow about her, Deedee decided, that so many pregnant women had. She'd just started to wear maternity clothes, and Forrest had bought her the cute top she was wearing that said Baby Under Construction, which he'd proclaimed to be perfect for the wife of an architect.

Deedee's smile faded as her gaze fell on Ryan MacAllister. He was the second son, born between Michael and Forrest. She didn't know Ryan as well as the others, but she did know of the tragic loss of his wife more than a year and a half before. She'd met Sherry at the twins' christening, then had attended her funeral when she'd been slain by a berserk gunman at the hospital where she'd worked.

Since then, Ryan seemed to keep Deedee, as well as his family, at arm's length the majority of the time.

The family had been devastated by Sherry's violent death, then stunned when Ryan immediately resigned from the police force.

At the time, Andrea and Jillian had told Deedee that everyone was extremely worried about Ryan. He'd closed himself into the apartment where he'd lived with Sherry, and refused to allow anyone entry. For the entire month following his wife's death, he drank heavily, emerging only to buy food and more liquor.

At their wit's end, Michael, Forrest and Ted Sharpe, Ryan's former police partner, had gone to Ryan's and threatened to break the door down if he didn't let them in.

When Ryan finally opened the door, they discovered a Ryan who was alarmingly thin and haggard, with wild hair and a bushy beard. The apartment was a mess and reeked of alcohol. Ryan was angry at their intrusion and demanded to be left alone.

By brute force, he was thrown in the shower, told to put on fresh clothes, then hauled to a barbershop for a shave and haircut. The trio then took a fuming Ryan to a restaurant, ordered him a big meal and announced he wasn't leaving until he'd consumed the food.

While he was away from his apartment with his self-appointed rescuers, the women of the family had swooped in to clean, polish, wash clothes and stock the refrigerator.

Ted Sharpe had then threatened to stay at Ryan's, sleeping on the sofa, and not leave until Ryan came up with a plan of action, a concrete decision as to what he was going to do with his life.

More out of desperation to be left alone than desire, Ryan had started his own business, MacAllister Security Systems.

Andrea had recently told Deedee that Ryan's company was growing, and he now had a secretary as well as two installers. What none of the family knew, Andrea had said with a sad-sounding sigh, was whether or not Ryan was pleased with his new endeavor, or if he was even close to finding an inner peace and had come to terms with Sherry's death. The walls he'd erected around himself after Sherry died were solidly in place.

"These gifts are from Uncle Ted," Andrea said to the twins. "He's on duty today, but he wishes you both a happy, happy birthday."

"Happy burffday," Noel said, clapping her hands. She reached eagerly for one of the presents that Andrea held. "Mine."

"Mine," Matt said.

Andrea laughed and gave them the gifts. "They're really getting with the program here. John, are you remembering to take pictures? I want a record of everything for the family album."

"I'm not missing a thing," John said, holding the camera to one eye. "There will be pages and pages in the album titled Twins Turning Two."

The twins tore open the boxes from Ted and each pulled out a stuffed toy. Ted Sharpe had gotten them teddy bears dressed in police uniforms, one a girl teddy bear and one a boy. As the adults exclaimed over the cute toys, Deedee looked quickly at Ryan.

He was separate and apart from the others, having leaned one shoulder against a far wall and crossed his arms loosely over his chest.

As the teddy bears in the police garb appeared, a slight smile formed on his lips. He shifted his stance, and his eyes collided with hers.

Her breath caught as she saw him immediately change his expression to a closed, unreadable one, revealing nothing of what he was feeling.

She returned her attention to the giggling twins.

Ryan was an extremely handsome man, Deedee thought. He was thirty-six or thirty-seven, about six feet tall with thick brown hair and the MacAllister brown eyes. He was well built, with wide shoulders and nicely proportioned muscles. And according to Jillian, he now focused all his energies on MacAllister Security Systems.

But there was a cold aura to Ryan MacAllister, a hands-off, don't-get-too-close attitude emanating from him with such intensity it was a nearly palpable entity. She had seen him conceal his emotions the moment their eyes met. He had perfected the ability to drop solid walls around himself at will.

Ryan MacAllister would certainly turn women's heads when he entered a room, but Deedee had a sneaky suspicion that he wouldn't care about, or even notice, the feminine attention he was receiving. It was as though, Andrea had once told Deedee, the fun-loving, warm, charming Ryan had died with Sherry.

The family was saddened as they realized that the Ryan who had emerged from the month-long solitude was there to stay—aloof, empty and existing on not only the fringes of the family, but of life, as well.

Deedee shook her head slightly to bring her back to the activities around her.

Concentrating so intently on Ryan had, she realized, caused a gloomy feeling to settle over her, created by painful thoughts from her own past. She'd laid her ghosts to rest many years ago, and she would not allow Ryan's troubles to cause her dark memories to inch forward once again.

She needed to talk to him one-on-one, something she'd never done before. This party was an excellent opportunity to discuss with Ryan what was on her mind, but she now knew she'd have to be on emotional red alert. As coldhearted as it might sound, she'd have to make certain that Ryan's problems remained just that—his.

"On behalf of Noel and Matt," Andrea said, returning Deedee to the moment at hand, "I want to thank all of you for their lovely gifts."

"And the wrapping paper," John said, laughing as Matt shredded another piece. "Our son has a head for business. He's making confetti to sell next New Year's Eve."

"Cake and ice cream time," Andrea said. "Let's tromp back into the dining room, then you can bring your dessert in here where it's more comfortable."

"Great," Forrest said, rubbing his hands together. "We can play with the toys. These guys got some fascinating-looking stuff."

"Remember to share, Forrest," Jillian said, smiling at him. "There will be none of this 'mine' business from you. Let Noel and Matt have a turn."

"Yes, ma'am," he said, then dropped a quick kiss on her lips. "This is research, darling wife. You know how you have to do all that heavy-duty research for your books? Well, I have an assignment that will be part of my job description as a daddy. I have to be able to assemble and know how to play with a vast variety of toys."

"Ah, I see," Jillian said, nodding. "It's tough work, but a daddy has to do it, I guess. Your self-sacrifice is duly noted."

"One should hope," he said.

"The writing is on the wall, Margaret," Robert MacAllister said. "In the future when we buy a toy for Jillian and Forrest's little one, we'll have to get two—one for the baby, and one for Forrest."

"Now that," Forrest said, pointing one finger in the air, "is a fantastic idea."

Everyone was laughing and talking as they went into the dining room. Ryan, Deedee noted, seemed to be chatting pleasantly with his mother. As each was served, they wandered back into the living room.

Ryan settled onto the padded bench edging the inside of a bay window at one end of the room.

Go for it, Deedee told herself. This was a perfect chance to speak with Ryan. She simply had to remember not to allow his reality to intrude on hers.

She crossed the room and smiled as she stopped in front of him.

"May I join you, Ryan?"

His head snapped up. "What? Oh, sure thing, Deedee. There's plenty of space here."

She sat down, then shifted so she could look directly at him.

"The twins were so cute with their presents," she said. "I'll be eager to see the pictures John took."

Ryan nodded, then took a bite of cake.

Brother, Deedee thought crossly, he apparently doesn't intend to even attempt to make conversation. If he smiled, his face would probably crack due to it being so long since he'd done it.

She sampled her own cake.

Patience, Deedee, she thought. Stay cheerful. She would *not* allow this grumpy, gloomy man to dim her party mood.

"This cake is delicious," she said, then paused. "Ryan, do you mind talking business on a Sunday afternoon?"

He looked at her again and shrugged. "No."

She'd never been this near to him before, Deedee mused. He really was extremely handsome. His features were rugged and masculine, and she could smell just the faintest hint of musky after-shave.

His eyes, though, were disturbing. All the Mac-Allisters had warm and expressive brown eyes, but Ryan's were...flat—yes, that was the word—with no clue as to what he was thinking or feeling.

"Deedee?" he said, frowning slightly.

"Oh, I'm sorry. I was daydreaming for a minute. What I wanted to talk to you about was—"

"You have freckles," Ryan said suddenly. "I never noticed that before. They're dancing a jig right across your nose."

Lord, MacAllister, he thought, where had that come from? What a stupid thing to open his mouth and say. What difference did it make if Deedee Hamilton had freckles on her pert little nose? It was just that it was rather refreshing that she hadn't covered them with that makeup glop women used. She let them do the two-step on her nose for all the world to see.

Deedee blinked. "Well, yes, I have freckles on my nose. They've been there forever. In all the time you and I have known each other, I guess you've never been this close—" she laughed "—to my nose."

A shaft of unexpected heat rocketed through Ryan's body at the tinkling sound of Deedee's laughter. As though seeing her for the first time, he quickly cataloged her big, brown eyes, her short hair that was a fetching mass of strawberry blond curls and her delicate features.

Deedee Hamilton, he mused, was very pretty. She wasn't beautiful, or sophisticatedly stunning; she was pretty, in a wholesome, fresh-air-and-sunshine way. And he sure did like those cute freckles.

Why was he having this asinine conversation with himself? he wondered in self-disgust. He really didn't give a rip if Deedee had a polka-dotted nose and laughter like windchimes and... *Ah, hell, Mac-Allister, can it.*

Ryan cleared his throat and set his plate next to him on the cushion.

"You wanted to discuss business?" he said, looking at Deedee again.

She continued to smile. "Have we thoroughly exhausted the subject of my nose?"

Ryan smiled.

He couldn't help himself really, because Deedee's laughter was infectious and her smile beckoned to be matched by another one. Her brown eyes—the biggest brown eyes he'd ever seen—were sparkling, actually sparkling. The entire package that was Deedee was extremely appealing.

So he smiled.

And Deedee stopped breathing.

Dear heaven, she thought, then told herself to draw some air into her lungs before she passed out on her freckled nose. Ryan MacAllister's smile was a sight to behold. The stern set of his jaw relaxed, and the creases in his forehead smoothed, making him appear younger. His teeth were white and straight, and his lips were shaped so perfectly.

And those MacAllister brown eyes were now warm and inviting, like chocolate sauce a person would gladly drown in.

"You have a wonderful smile, Ryan," she said, hearing the thread of breathlessness in her voice. "You should use it more often. It's perfectly legal for me to express my opinion regarding your smile, since you commented on my freckled nose."

Ryan chuckled and nodded. "Tit for tat. Now we're even."

Oh, not fair, Deedee thought. That throaty chuckle was without a doubt one of the sexiest, most masculine sounds she'd ever heard. Her cheeks felt warm. If she was blushing because she couldn't ignore the purely feminine flutter in the pit of her stomach, she was going to die of embarrassment right there on the spot.

"You're blushing," Ryan said. "Did I miss something here?"

"No," she said quickly. "I'm not blushing. Well, yes, I guess I am, but that doesn't mean I have any legitimate *reason* to blush. Sometimes I just blush, which is very annoying, considering that I'm thirty-three years old, for crying out loud. Oh, good Lord, now I'm babbling." She waved one hand in the air. "Ignore me."

Ryan's smile faded. "That would be difficult to do, Deedee."

Their eyes met, and Deedee could hear the sudden increased tempo of her heart echoing in her ears.

Heat once again swept through Ryan's body, coiling deep and low within him. He told himself to tear his gaze from Deedee's, to stop looking at those remarkable brown eyes of hers, but he couldn't move.

Damn it, he fumed, what kind of spell weaver was she? What was she doing to him? Well, he wasn't interested—not in her, or any woman, for that matter.

"Attention, folks," Forrest yelled. "I need your undivided attention, one and all."

Deedee and Ryan jerked at the sudden intrusive noise of Forrest's booming voice. They snapped their heads around to stare at Forrest standing in the middle of the room.

Bless you, Forrest, Deedee thought. Ryan MacAllister was a dangerous man. There was just something, a blatantly masculine and sensual *something*, about him that was compelling, nearly overpowering. She wanted no part of it, whatever it was. No.

"All right, here it is," Forrest said, rubbing his hands together. "The topic is The Baby Bet."

"Oh, good grief," Jillian said, rolling her eyes heavenward.

"You're a tad early," Michael said. "Well, whatever. Okay, I bet that Jillian *is* going to have a baby. I win. Give me some money."

"Cork it, Michael," Forrest said. "This is serious business. I am, as all of you know, The Baby Bet champion. I won when Bobby was born *and* when the twins arrived. It's only fair to warn you that I've since won The Baby Bet with the mailman, a couple I designed a house for, *and* one of Jillian's author friends. Simply put, I can't be beat." He nodded decisively, a smug expression on his face.

"Margaret," Robert MacAllister said, "where did we go wrong raising that one?"

"I have no idea," she said, patting her husband's knee. "He certainly is full of himself, isn't he?"

Forrest glared at his parents. "I'm stating facts here, Mr. and Mrs. MacAllister. I *am* The Baby Bet champion."

"Yes, dear," his mother said. "I do believe the whole world knows that by now."

"I should hope so," Forrest said.

"It's time to unchampion you," Michael said. "Is that a word?"

Jillian laughed. "I don't think so."

"Okay, big shot," John said. "What's the deal?"

"I'm glad you asked," Forrest said. "Now pay attention, people, because this one is going to be complicated."

"Jillian," Andrea said, "are you going to strangle him, or run him down with your car?"

"Could I have some respect here?" Forrest hollered.

"No!" John and Michael yelled in unison.

"No, no, no," Noel said merrily.

"Hush, sweetheart," Andrea said. "Your Uncle Forrest is slipping over the edge."

"What a group," Forrest said, shaking his head.

What a *wonderful* group, Deedee thought, laughing softly. Oh, how she adored this family. They were warm, loving, funny and fun.

Ryan slid a quick glance at Deedee.

Her eyes were sparkling again, he mused. She was enjoying the crazy antics of his family to the max. Deedee was a widow. Yeah, he remembered that now.

Her husband had been killed many years ago, though he didn't recall the details of how it had happened. She was alone and had adopted, per se, the MacAllisters as her family.

Why would a pretty, vivacious, refreshing woman like Deedee Hamilton still be alone? Ryan wondered. Oh, hell, what difference did it make? It was none of his business. He really didn't care. But then again, it didn't make sense. Why was Deedee still alone?

"If you're done being dumb," Forrest said, "I'll explain the program. Jillian is having an ultrasound on Wednesday. Therefore, The Baby Bet is high-tech. It includes not only the questions of is it a boy or a girl? One? Twins? But also the stand that they won't be able to tell the sex because the munchkin was modest and stayed curled up. Get it?"

"Ah-h-h," Michael said, stroking his chin. "I like this one. It has pizzazz. Whip out your paper and pencil, Forrest. I'm ready."

Forrest took a small pad of paper and a pen from his shirt pocket.

"Go for it, Michael," he said, "and get ready to kiss your twenty bucks goodbye."

"Says you," Michael said. "Okay, here's my prediction. Jillian is having twins. That's a given, because she's getting very fat, very fast."

"*Him* I'll strangle," Jillian said.

"I'll bet," Michael said, staring at the ceiling, "a girl and an unknown. They won't be able to tell the sex of the second one."

"Got it," Forrest said, writing on the pad.

"No, no way. It's just one big boy," John said.

"One girl," Ryan said, "who will take after Jillian, because the world isn't ready for another Forrest."

Forrest looked at him in surprise. "You want in on The Baby Bet?"

"Yeah, why not?" Ryan said. More to the question...why? He hadn't interacted with his family's nonsense since... Well, The Baby Bet was no big deal. It was sort of fun. What the hell, why not? "I don't mind taking your money, Forrest."

"Not a chance. All right, you're in. Dad? What about you?"

"Well, it seems to me," Robert said, "that we should be told the champion's bet. I want to know where your money is going, Forrest, before I decide on mine."

"Clever man," Forrest said. "No wonder we all turned out so terrific. You're a smart person."

"Spill it," Ryan said. "What's your bet?"

"Ladies and gentleman," Forrest said, "the champion, and the planning-to-remain champion, is hereby placing his twenty dollars on girls." He paused, sweeping his gaze over the group, then grinned at Jillian. "Three of them!"

"What?" Jillian said, jumping to her feet. "Forrest MacAllister, don't you dare say such a thing out loud. With your uncanny knack for winning The Baby Bet..." She sank back onto her chair and pressed her hands to her cheeks. "Oh, my stars."

"Twins run in the family," Margaret said thoughtfully, "so I suppose it's reasonable that there might be... Goodness gracious."

Deedee looked at Ryan with wide eyes.

"Triplets?" she said. "No, that's crazy. You don't think he's right, do you, Ryan?"

Ryan chuckled and shrugged, realizing to his own amazement that he was actually enjoying himself.

"Forrest is the champion," he said, still smiling. "He hasn't been wrong so far."

"Do you realize," Deedee said, "how many diapers a person would change in one given day if they had three babies?"

"Quite a few."

"No, no, no," Jillian said to no one in particular. "I refuse. That's it. Nope. I'm not having triplets, three baby girls at one time. No, no, no."

"No, no, no," Noel said, clapping her hands.

"Thank you, Noel," Jillian said. "I appreciate your support."

"Wednesday night," Forrest said, "we'll all meet at Mario's for pizza at seven o'clock to hear the results of the test, and to announce the winner of The Baby Bet. Me."

"This time you're going to lose," Jillian said. "Please, Forrest?"

Everyone started talking at once about Forrest's outrageous prediction.

"Well, Deedee," Ryan said, "will you be at Mario's to see how this comes out?"

"I certainly will." She paused. "Are you planning to go?"

Ryan started to automatically reply in the negative, then hesitated.

What the hell, why not?

"Yes," he said, looking directly into her eyes. "Yes, I'll be there."

Chapter Two

Before Deedee could comment on Ryan having confirmed that he would be joining everyone for pizza, a buzzing noise sounded.

"Excuse me," Ryan said.

He reached for a small black box that was clipped to the side of his belt. Numbers were moving across a half-inch viewing bar near the top of the device. He nodded, pressed a button to erase the numbers, then slid the box back onto his belt.

"That doesn't surprise me," he said, looking at Deedee again. "I've got my guys working overtime today on a system the customer wanted put in five minutes after he decided to get it. I told my men to give me a holler if they had any problems." He got to his feet. "They obviously have a problem. If you'll excuse me, Deedee, I'll go telephone them."

"Yes, of course."

Deedee watched as Ryan walked across the room, indulging herself in a thorough scrutiny of his very nice tush. He also, she mused, moved with the smooth, athletic grace of a man in excellent physical condition, who was comfortable in his body. She'd never noticed that before.

Good buns, she reaffirmed in her mind, then scolded herself in the next instant for being naughty.

Actually, she was glad that Ryan had been removed from her presence at the moment he had been. Now she would simply refuse to discuss with herself the rush of pleasure that had swept through her when he had said he would be joining everyone for pizza on Wednesday night. Her reaction had been ridiculous and unexplainable. She would, therefore, ignore it.

"I have to go," Ryan announced to the group when he reappeared in the room. "There's a snag on a hurry-up job we're doing, and my crew needs an extra pair of hands." He tousled Noel's hair, then Matt's. "Happy birthday. Check your Uncle Forrest's pockets before he leaves to be sure he doesn't have any of your new toys."

Ryan thanked Andrea and John for the great party, hugged his mother, then looked over at Deedee.

"It was nice talking to you, Deedee," he said from the center of the room. "I'll be seeing you."

She smiled and nodded.

I'll be seeing you, too, she thought, on Wednesday night at Mario's. *Oh, Deedee, for Pete's sake, cut it out.*

As soon as Ryan had left the house, Andrea made a beeline for Deedee and plunked down next to her on the window seat.

"Deedee Hamilton," Andrea said, beaming, "what did you do to my brother?"

"Do?" Deedee repeated, obviously confused.

"Yes, 'do.' Ryan was smiling, laughing . . . was enjoying himself. I know he was. Plus, he took part in The Baby Bet. He was, here, in this very room, sitting next to you, more like the old Ryan than he has been since Sherry died. So I repeat. What did you do?"

"Nothing," she said, laughing. "You're acting as though I cast a spell over him, or sprinkled magic dust on his cake, or something. We were simply chatting. I didn't urge him to participate in The Baby Bet. He just opened his mouth and did it."

"Amazing," Andrea said, shaking her head. "And wonderful, believe me. Everyone noticed that he was more relaxed, easygoing . . . well, more like he used to be than we've seen him behave in nearly two years. *You* definitely had a hand in that."

"Andrea," Deedee said, narrowing her eyes, "pay attention to what I'm about to say. Don't you dare get into your Cupid mode in regard to me and Ryan. I am *not* interested."

Andrea splayed one hand on her chest. "Would I do that? Play Cupid? Me?"

"Don't pull your all-innocent routine on me. I was your partner in crime in Cupidville when we got Jillian and Forrest together. Remember? I recognize that gleam in your eyes, because we both had it back then when we thought we were hotshot Cupids. We came very close to creating a total disaster, if you'll recall."

Andrea sighed. "I know. It almost backfired big time." She smiled again. "But it turned out all right. Do note that our Jillian and Forrest are as happy as two bugs in a rug."

"Andrea, do *not* try to be a matchmaker between me and Ryan. Promise?"

"Oh...do I have to?"

"Yes, because I know you'd never break a promise."

"Well, darn." Andrea paused. "Okay, I promise under protest. It's a shame, because you obviously had a marvelous influence on Ryan."

"You're reading too much into it. He allowed *himself* to have a good time today. It had nothing to do with me. I wouldn't get too excited about it so you won't be disappointed. It may have been an isolated incident that won't happen again."

"That's true, I suppose. It breaks my heart to continually see how much he's changed, how closed he is, aloof. He built walls around himself when Sherry died. I wish he'd... Oh, I've been through this wish list a thousand times."

"I know you have, Andrea. You all love him and want him to be happy again. The thing is, you can't heal his wounds for him. He has to do it himself."

"But what if he doesn't, Deedee? It's been nearly two years already. Well, it was wonderful to see him smile today, hear him laugh. Wouldn't it be something if he showed up for pizza Wednesday night? No, I'm dreaming. He only joins the family for special occasions. He wouldn't come for The Baby Bet nonsense of Forrest's."

Deedee started to speak, then decided against it. There was no point in telling Andrea that Ryan had said he *would* be attending the gathering at Mario's. There was every chance that he'd change his mind, and it wouldn't be kind to get Andrea's hopes up.

"Oh, darn," Deedee said, her eyes widening.

"What's wrong?"

"I never got a chance to talk to Ryan about the security system for Books and Books. I'd like him to give me an estimate on what it would cost to install a better system than the landlord provides. According to my lease, I can do it at my own expense. I have over two hundred rare books now, in addition to my regular stock. I need to protect them better against theft."

"Call Ryan tomorrow," Andrea said, studying her fingernails. "Ask him to stop by the store." She looked at Deedee and smiled. "Then invite him out to dinner."

"Andrea," Deedee said, a warning tone to her voice, "you promised. Erase the word Cupid from your brain."

"You're no fun."

"Tough toasties."

"Deedee, speaking of Wednesday at Mario's for pizza, are you coming?"

"Sure."

"Good. Oh, my, can you believe what Forrest predicted? Three baby girls? Triplets? My twins keep me hopping, let me tell you. I can't imagine having three. No, Forrest is wrong. He may be The Baby Bet champion, but he's about to be—what did Michael say?— oh, yes, unchampioned."

"I wouldn't be so certain of that, Andrea. Jillian is getting quite a tummy for only being four months' pregnant. That's why the doctor wants to do the ultrasound. Plus, Forrest has had a perfect score up to now. He has an uncanny knack, it seems, for winning The Baby Bet."

"Oh, my," Andrea said, shaking her head. "It boggles the mind."

"I wouldn't miss that pizza party Wednesday for anything," Deedee said. "I want to hear the results of that test."

"Mmm," Andrea said, tapping one fingertip against her chin. "I wonder if Ryan will be there?"

"Oh, good night," Deedee said, rolling her eyes heavenward.

Would Ryan actually come? she mused. *Deedee Hamilton, that is enough.* She was as bad as Andrea. The subject of Ryan's attendance, or nonattendance, at Mario's was a closed and forgotten topic. If he showed up...fine. If not...no big deal. Then again, he *did* say that he planned to be there and...

"Oh-h-h," Deedee said with a moan. She was driving herself crazy.

"What's your problem?" Andrea said, blinking in surprise at Deedee's outburst.

"Problem? Oh. My problem." She jumped to her feet. "I was trying to talk myself out of having another piece of cake, but I lost the battle." She sighed dramatically. "More calories, here I come."

"You don't have to watch your weight," Andrea said, frowning. "You eat whatever you want to and don't gain an ounce. You're greenly envied by the general female populace."

"Oh, well, yes, but one never knows when one's metabolism might change. I may turn into a Pillsbury Dough Girl before your very eyes. Too bad. I'm off to get more cake."

"Pillsbury Dough Girl?" Andrea said, laughing as Deedee marched away. "If Forrest is right, I'm afraid it's Jillian who's going to have that dubious honor."

Ryan jerked upward in bed and drew a deep, ragged breath. His heart was pounding wildly, and beads of sweat dotted his forehead. He shook his head, hoping to dispel the lingering fogginess of sleep *and* the images of the disturbing dream he'd had.

The clock on the nightstand glowed 2:12 a.m. With a groan, he sank back onto the pillow, wishing it was closer to dawn so he could leave the bed and begin the day.

He did *not* want to run the risk of drifting off to sleep again and having the dream pick up where it had left off.

Damn it, he fumed, dragging both hands down his face. *He'd dreamed about Deedee Hamilton.* It had been so real, not one of those mishmash dreams that made no sense.

Oh, it had made sense, all right. Deedee had been standing in front of him in a vivid field of wildflowers, wearing a pink gauze dress. The sky was a brilliant blue, and a dozen beautiful butterflies had been fluttering through the air above her head.

She had lifted her slender hands in an enticingly feminine and graceful motion, as though to touch the elusive butterflies.

And then she'd laughed—in delight, the enchanting sound causing desire to course through him like a roaring current rushing out of control.

In the dream, he'd reached for her, wanting her, aching for her, burning. Just as his hand grazed her arm, she twirled away, her laughter lilting through the flower-scented air.

"I'm a butterfly, Ryan," she called. "Catch me if you can."

He matched her smile. "And if I do?"

"Then I'll be yours. We'll make love, here, in the beautiful flowers beneath the blue sky. The butterflies will protect us from outsiders. There will be only the two of us, together. Forever, Ryan. Forever, forever, forever."

Ryan threw back the blankets, left the bed, then strode naked from the bedroom to the kitchen. He turned on the light, squinting against the bright glare. Moving to the sink, he drank a glass of water, then thudded the glass onto the counter.

Gripping the edge of the sink so tightly his knuckles were white, he stared unseeing at his own reflection in the dark window in front of him.

A painful knot twisted in his gut and he welcomed it, acknowledged it as his due for having had a sensual dream about a woman other than Sherry.

He mentally scrambled for Sherry's image, wanting it front-row center in his mind's eye. *But it wouldn't come. He couldn't see it.* Every corner of his brain held pictures of Deedee.

Deedee smiling. Laughing. Dancing with the butterflies. Beckoning to him.

Promising him forever.

"Damn it," he said.

He made a fist and slammed it on the counter, pain shooting up his arm like a hot arrow.

"Oh, hell," he said, clutching his fist with his other hand. "Man, oh, man, that hurts."

Turning on the faucet, he held the throbbing hand under cold water, swearing a blue streak in self-disgust.

Why? he asked himself. Why in the name of heaven had he dreamed something like that about Deedee Hamilton? He hadn't looked at another woman since Sherry had been killed. To him, their wedding vows were still firmly in place. He was married to Sherry, and he would be until the day he died. *Death was the only forever that was guaranteed.*

But, dear God, he couldn't see Sherry's face!

In one of his drunken rages following her death, he'd destroyed every picture he'd had of her, unable to bear the agony of looking at the woman he loved, knowing he would never hold her, kiss her, make love to her again.

He'd later regretted his rash action, but what was done was done. He had the image of Sherry in crystal clarity in his mind, and that would hold him in good stead.

And it had.

Until now.

Until this horrifying, guilt-ridden night, when he'd dreamed of another woman, of Deedee. And the damnable blue sky and butterflies.

As his hand began to grow numb from the icy cold water, he smacked off the faucet and reached for the towel slipped through the handle of the refrigerator.

A few minutes later he returned to bed, staring up at a ceiling he couldn't see in the darkness.

Get a grip, MacAllister, he ordered himself. So okay, the dream had shaken him, made him feel like a scum, but it *was* only a dream. But weren't dreams supposedly messages of truth from a person's subconscious? Hell, he didn't know. He was a cop, not a shrink.

Oh, great, terrific, just dandy. He'd just mentally referred to himself as a cop, something he hadn't been for nearly two years. Where had *that* come from?

Easy, MacAllister, you're losing it.

He had to calm down, sort this through, determine what was going on.

Deedee.

He'd known her for years, but today at the twins' birthday party was the first occasion he'd ever really talked to her. In the past he'd done the usual "Hello. How are you? Goodbye" routine at family gatherings. Today they'd had an actual conversation, face-to-face.

And Deedee had freckles on her nose.

Ryan muttered an earthy expletive and told himself to forget about the freckles on Deedee Hamilton's nose. Her nose was not the issue. What was important here was what in the hell that woman had done to him in the short time they'd sat together on the window seat. Sat *close* together, very close.

Actually, now that he thought about it, he'd acted rather weird during the entire birthday party. For reasons he couldn't fathom, he'd taken part in The Baby Bet, told Deedee he'd be joining the group for pizza on Wednesday night and had relaxed and enjoyed the twins' party.

Strange, very strange.

Well, that was fine. His unusual behavior had produced a loving and happy smile on his mother's face. It hadn't strained his brain to be a little more sociable for a change. So okay, that settled that part of this confusing maze.

Which brought him right back to Deedee.

Deedee Hamilton had not been the *cause* of his enjoying the celebration, rather she had been a *result* of his unexpected attitude. He let down his guard, and she'd skittered into place right in front of him, complete with the cutest freckled nose and the biggest brown eyes he'd ever seen.

Ryan released a sigh of relief. There, he'd figured it all out. He hadn't been disloyal to Sherry, not really. Now that he had the facts, everything would fall back into place as it should be. He'd see Sherry clearly in his mind's eye, remember the sound of her laughter and the feel of her lips on his.

"Yes," he said, decisively.

He rolled onto his stomach, closed his eyes and, moments later, was asleep.

But when Ryan awoke hours later, his fury returned in full force.

The first thought he'd had, the first vision he'd seen in his mind when he woke up, had been of Deedee.

Chapter Three

"Here you are," Deedee said, handing a woman a plastic bag. "I hope you enjoy the books."

"Oh, I will," the woman said, smiling. "My husband has gone to a business conference for three days in Colorado. I plan to light a fire in the hearth, curl up with my cat and a warm afghan and not budge. These books will be the frosting on my 'it's my turn for me' cake."

"That sounds marvelous," Deedee said, returning the woman's smile.

"Don't misunderstand me, dear. I love my husband every bit, if not more, than when I married him thirty-six years ago. But I've learned that if I indulge myself, pamper myself, when he goes away like this,

my emotional batteries get recharged. And I'm so very
glad to see him when he arrives home."

"You're a wise woman," Deedee said, nodding.

"My dear," she said, laughing, "I truly believe that
women in general are far wiser than men. Well, goodbye for now."

"Goodbye."

A frown replaced Deedee's smile as she watched the
woman leave the store.

Thirty-six years, she mused. When that woman had
spoken of her husband coming home, love had shone
in her eyes, on her face. That couple had been married longer than she, herself, had been on this earth.
Incredible. What would it be like to literally spend a
lifetime with a man, a soul mate? How glorious it must
be to have a forever with a special someone.

Deedee shook her head slightly in self-disgust.

Where were these strange thoughts coming from?
During the years since her husband, Jim, had been
killed, she'd intentionally avoided any serious relationships with men. She'd considered her options
carefully, weighed and measured, sifted and sorted,
and decided never to remarry.

What she'd shared with Jim, albeit for a short time,
had been rare and beautiful. Love like that, she was
convinced, didn't happen twice. Rather than settle for
less than what she'd had, she had focused on starting
her own business with Jim's insurance money.

She was a dedicated career woman, and had been
for a long time. Her life-style suited her perfectly, and
she was content and fulfilled. She dated regularly, had

wonderful friends and even a family in the form of the MacAllister clan.

Her own parents had passed away within months of each other seven years ago. She'd been widowed for three years then, and the loss of her parents had been devastating. Once again she'd had to reach deep within herself for the strength to cope with her grief.

Why was she dwelling on the past today? Deedee wondered. She really didn't know, but she'd felt a strange chill of loneliness within her as the customer had spoken of the love for her husband of thirty-six years.

Loneliness? That was absurd. Deedee was *not* lonely. She wasn't a single woman by default, but by choice. She had her existence established exactly the way she wanted it. The MacAllisters were even adding more babies to the ever-growing family, babies she could spoil rotten in her role of Aunt Deedee.

No, that hadn't really been loneliness she'd registered, it was merely fatigue. She was exhausted, because she hadn't slept well the night before. It was very unusual for her to toss and turn, but she'd spent a restless night, only dozing, then waking again. No, she hadn't slept well at all because . . .

Deedee sighed.

Because she'd been thinking about Ryan Mac-Allister.

There, she'd admitted it.

She glanced at the clock on the wall.

It had taken her until 1:16 in the afternoon to square off against the ridiculous truth, but now she'd done it.

She'd been consumed through the seemingly endless night by thoughts and images of Ryan.

Like a silly teenager, she'd been unable to keep herself from replaying in her mind every moment she'd spent with Ryan at the twins' birthday party.

"Dumb," she said under her breath.

She retrieved a dust cloth from beneath the counter and marched across the room to dust books that didn't need dusting.

Because of her asinine performance of the night before, she'd been reluctant to telephone Ryan's office today to make an appointment with him to come to Books and Books and determine the best security system to protect her collection of rare books.

She now realized she'd been harboring the irrational idea that if she came face-to-face with Ryan, he'd instantly know that her mind had been centered on him through the night.

Even worse, she'd somehow telegraph to him the fact that more than once during those hours she'd experienced the heated thrum of desire pulsing low in her body.

"Dumb, dumb, dumb," she said to a cookbook. "He'd never know how infantile I'd been."

Well, now wait a minute.

She stopped, holding the dust cloth in midair and staring into space.

Maybe she was being too hard on herself. It was...healthy—yes, she liked that conclusion—that she had a normal, womanly, although a tad wanton, reaction to an extremely handsome, virile, masculinity-personified man.

As long as she didn't tear her clothes off and leap into Ryan's arms when she saw him again, she decided with a smile, there was no harm done. Her restless night simply reaffirmed that she was alive and kicking. Healthy.

The next encounter with Ryan would prove without a doubt that she was over her momentary female-to-male reaction to him, and everything would be status quo.

She was perfectly fine *now,* as a matter of fact, and would confirm that knowledge by telephoning him at his office as she should have done the moment she arrived at the store that morning.

With a decisive nod and the self-assurance that she'd logically explained and could therefore dismiss her bizarre and sleepless night, Deedee started back across the room, her destination being the telephone.

When she was within four feet of the counter, the door opened, accompanied by the tinkling of the brass bell above it. She turned with a smile to greet the customer, then froze, the smile disappearing into oblivion.

Ryan MacAllister had just entered Books and Books.

Ryan closed the door, but didn't move forward. Their eyes met. Neither spoke.

Ah, damn, Ryan fumed. His grand plan had just gone up in the smoke being created by the heated desire rocketing through him.

After being wired and edgy the entire morning, and *still* unable to dismiss Deedee Hamilton from his mind, he'd decided to confront her in person. The encounter, he was certain, would get him safely back on track. Deedee would once again become the friendly, attractive woman he'd known for several years, with no major role or impact whatsoever on his life.

He had a legitimate excuse to come to Books and Books. Deedee had expressed the wish to discuss business with him, but he'd been called away before they'd talked about what was on her agenda. He was being an efficient executive by following through on her request.

So there he was, standing in her store, fully prepared to breathe a sigh of relief that whatever nonsense had possessed him during the hideous night before was actually long since gone.

Instead...? His blood was pounding in his veins, his heart was beating like a bongo drum and he had a nearly overpowering urge to cross the room, haul Deedee into his arms and kiss her senseless.

Damn it to hell, what was this woman doing to him?

A deep frown settled over Ryan's features as he swept his gaze around the spacious, attractive store.

"Nice place," he said gruffly.

Deedee gave herself a mental shake, ordered her heart to slow its racing pace and plastered what she hoped would appear to be a normal friendly smile on her face.

Suddenly remembering her irrational thought that Ryan would be able to peer into her brain and see how she'd spent the night, she blushed. The warm flush on her cheeks caused her to silently moan in embarrassment.

Oh, Deedee, she begged herself, *please get it together.*

"Hello?" Ryan said.

"Oh. Thank you for the compliment about the store. I'm very proud of Books and Books."

She hurried across the room, deciding to put the counter between her and Ryan, hoping to feel less vulnerable and exposed.

"I was just going to call you, Ryan," she said, smiling brightly. "You must have been reading my mind." Oh, good grief, what a dumb thing to say. He'd better *not* be reading her mind. "I appreciate your coming by."

"You said at the twins' party that you wanted to discuss business," he said with no hint of a smile, "but we didn't have a chance to do so." He shrugged. "So here I am, ready to discuss business."

Yes, Deedee thought, there he was, gorgeous as all get-out *and* grumpy. There was no evidence of the warm, friendly, relaxed Ryan of yesterday emanating from the man standing before her now. If this was his business demeanor, it was a miracle that he had so many customers. Well, fine. Two could play at this game.

"I wish to have a cost estimate done," she said, lifting her chin, "on an upgraded security system. As you can see, I've had cabinets custom-made with locks and wired glass to protect my rare books. The landlord has installed an alarm system that sets off a siren if exterior doors or windows are forced open.''

"Mmm,'' Ryan said, nodding. He walked slowly across the room to stand opposite her at the counter. "Let me guess. All the shops on this block have the same system, and they go off at the slightest provocation. For example, if a heavy truck is driven down the street. No one pays any attention to the sirens because of all the false alerts.''

"That's correct.'' She folded her hands primly on top of the counter. "My rare-book collection has grown considerably over the past few years and is very valuable. I want to protect those books more effectively and efficiently.''

Ryan narrowed his eyes. "Is there some reason you're talking like a schoolteacher lecturing a classroom full of kids who aren't paying much attention? You sound stuffy as hell.''

"Well, I beg your humble pardon,'' she said, planting her hands on her hips. "I was merely matching the tone you set when you came through that door. Not stuffy, Mr. MacAllister. Grumpy.''

"Grumpy?'' he repeated, then laughed in spite of himself. "Now *that* is a great word.'' He shook his head, still smiling. "Grumpy.''

The rich timbre of Ryan's oh-so-male laughter had the now-familiar effect on Deedee, and she felt the rush of heat swirling within her. While she'd decided her feminine reaction to Ryan's masculinity was healthy, it was becoming extremely unsettling and definitely annoying.

"Yes, well," she said, poking her nose in the air, "you *were* grumpy when you arrived. You were not in a frame of mind befitting a professional businessman."

"Want a sample of my cop mode?" he said, grinning. "I could give you a demonstration of my 'Up against the wall, scum,' that goes far beyond grumpy."

"No," she said, unable to curb her bubbling laughter any longer. "I'll pass on that one, thank you."

They continued to look at each other, sharing their smiles and savoring the warmth of the moment. Then slowly, so slowly, their smiles faded as the sensuality simmering beneath the warmth grew stronger, weaving around and through them, changing the comforting warmth into licking flames of heated desire.

Deedee's breasts were heavy, achy, yearning for a soothing caress. Her heart was pounding, and somewhere in her hazy mind she had the irrational thought that surely Ryan could hear its rapid tempo.

Everything seemed magnified, heightened. She was strangely aware of the feel of the soft curls of her hair against her cheeks and neck, of the gentle slope of her hips and buttocks and of the pulsing heat deep within her femininity.

From a source unknown, a little voice began to whisper to her, gaining volume as it insisted on being heeded.

Deedee, wake up. Ryan is dangerous. He's a threat to your peace of mind and the path you've chosen to walk in your life. Wake up.

She tore her gaze from his and took a step backward, wrapping her hands around her elbows in a protective gesture.

Ryan shook his head slightly to dispel the lingering, passion-laden fog that had consumed his sense of reality. He had been thrown off-kilter by Deedee Hamilton yet again. He knew it, and didn't like the fact, not one damn bit. He was, to quote Ms. Hamilton, now definitely grumpy.

"Hell," he said, running a restless hand over the back of his neck. "This is nuts. We're rather old to be experiencing hormone wars and unbridled lust. Enough is enough here."

Lust? Deedee's mind echoed. What an awful, unappealing word to describe the sensations she'd felt. Ryan was frowning again, retreating behind his walls, being grumpy to the max.

Lust? Ryan was right, of course, she mused on. That's all it could be, as there certainly weren't any romantic emotions involved in what kept happening between them. This was a classic case of chemical attraction, or some such thing. But wasn't there a more gentle word than lust?

"Did you hear what I said, Deedee?" Ryan said. "I don't want any part of..." He stopped speaking for a moment, searching his mind for a suitable description, then giving up the futile attempt. "I don't want any part of whatever this is!"

"You don't have to yell about it," she said, glaring at him.

"Sorry," he mumbled.

"Unbridled lust," she said with a cluck of disgust. "You're so eloquent, Mr. MacAllister."

"Well, what would *you* call it?" he said, matching her glower.

"I don't know. But I wouldn't describe it with something as tacky as *lust*."

"This," he said, pointing one long finger at her, "is an asinine conversation."

"Don't point that thing at me, it has a nail in it." She paused. "That was a joke, Ryan. You know, those funny little things people say so that other people will smile? Oh, forget it. You probably used up a year's quota of smiles at the twins' party, and now you're stuck on automatic grumpy, sullen, cold . . . all of the above."

"That's a lousy thing to say," he protested.

"It's right up there with 'unbridled lust,' mister."

Ryan opened his mouth to retort, then closed it again. When he finally spoke, there was a nondescript expression on his face and his voice had a pleasant tone to it.

"I can't help wondering," he said, "what that customer who's around the corner there is thinking about this chat we're having."

Deedee's eyes widened in horror and her hands flew to her cheeks.

"Oh, no," she whispered. "Don't tell me there's someone in here. I could have sworn I was alone when you arrived. Oh, my word, how embarrassing. Ryan, please say it isn't true."

He leaned toward her. "It isn't true," he said, matching her whisper for whisper.

"You rat," she said with a burst of laughter. "I believed you."

"You bought it, all right," he said, chuckling. "Even the freckles on your nose were blushing." He paused. "Deedee, look, let's start over. I just now came into the store. Okay? I'm here to discuss the possibility of upgrading your security system. As for the other... Well, we'll forget it. It won't happen again. It wasn't important. Agreed?"

Deedee nodded, while telling herself that what Ryan had just said made perfect sense, and was the best solution for moving past what had transpired between them. She was *not* registering a sense of disappointment at his having said, "It wasn't important." No, of course, she wasn't. It was just that... *Oh, Deedee, shut up.*

"Deedee, do you agree?"

"What? Oh, yes, certainly." She waved one hand breezily in the air. "As you said, it wasn't important." She cleared her throat. "Now then, let's talk about protecting me from..." *You!* "What I mean is, protecting my rare books and keeping them from being stolen."

"Right. First I need to look at the system you have now, then go from there. I want to check the electrical box. Where's your back door?"

Before Deedee could reply, a woman in her sixties entered the store.

"Hello," Deedee said, smiling. "May I help you find something, or would you prefer to browse?"

"I'm looking for a book on butterflies," the woman said. "It's for my grandson, who is about to celebrate his tenth birthday. He's fascinated by butterflies."

"Let me show you what we have in the children's section," Deedee said. "Ryan, the back door is through the storeroom, around the corner there."

"I'll find it," he said.

Ryan watched as Deedee came from behind the counter, then joined the woman. As the pair walked across the room, he let out a pent-up breath.

Butterflies? he mentally fumed. A woman comes into the store at exactly that moment and wants a book about butterflies?

Damn, the dream he'd had about Deedee the night before was rolling across his mental vision like a movie he had no way to stop.

There was Deedee, dancing with the butterflies. There was Deedee, looking like a vision of loveliness. There was Deedee, beckoning to him.

I'm a butterfly, Ryan. Catch me if you can. Then I'll be yours. We'll make love, here, in the beautiful flowers beneath the blue sky. There will be only the two of us, together. Forever, Ryan. Forever, forever, forever.

Ah, man, he thought, dragging both hands down his face. Deedee Hamilton was driving him crazy. He had to get out of the store and away from that woman.

With heavy steps, he strode to the storeroom, taking a small notebook and a pen from his shirt pocket as he went. He entered the storeroom and closed the door behind him.

Deedee slid a glance in the direction Ryan had gone, then redirected her attention to the woman next to her after he disappeared from view.

"Why don't I leave you to look through the various books on butterflies at your leisure?" Deedee said. "I'll be at the counter if you have any questions."

"That's fine," the woman said pleasantly. "Thank you so much."

Deedee hurried away, willing her trembling legs to get her to the stool behind the counter. Safely seated, she drew a steadying breath.

Ryan MacAllister, she thought, narrowing her eyes, was a menace. She wanted him out of her store and far away from her. He pushed sensual buttons within her that she didn't even know she possessed.

It wasn't important.

Have you got that yet, Deedee Hamilton? she thought angrily. *She* was in control of her life. *She* decided on the boundaries when she was involved with someone. If a man wanted a serious commitment from her, *she* sent him shuffling off to Buffalo. Men did *not* dictate to her in the areas of emotional and physical responses.

Nice spiel, she thought dryly. Her little mental speech was true, had been for years. Then Ryan MacAllister had come into her life and wreaked havoc with her program.

No, now wait a minute. It was even worse than that, more ridiculous and unexplainable.

Ryan had not *just* come into her life, he'd been there for several years. She'd known him, spoken to him, seen his gorgeous self, watched him interact with his family. He wasn't a complete stranger who appeared on her doorstep and threw her for a loop.

So why, why, why was she suddenly having a sexual response to him?

Oh, good grief, she didn't know. Didn't have a clue. Forget her conclusion that it was healthy. Absurd was closer to the mark. She was a mental mess, and had to formulate a plan for handling this nonsense.

She squinted at the ceiling.

When a person caught a cold, she mused, they had to resign themself to the fact that there was nothing they could do but let it run its course. They could take precautions, such as getting plenty of rest and drinking juice, but the cold was going to diminish, then finally disappear, in its own sweet time.

"Therefore," she said aloud, pointing one finger in the air. She was going to consider her reactions to Ryan as she would the common cold. Her uncharacteristic behavior and responses were simply going to have to be allowed to run their course. She obviously couldn't order them into oblivion any more than she could the sniffles.

Precautions could and would be taken. Oh, my, yes. She'd make sure she wasn't alone with Ryan, and she'd stay on alert and in complete touch with herself. Her sudden *awareness* of Ryan as a man, rather than just another MacAllister, would dim, flicker, then— poof—be gone.

And that, thank you very much, would be that.

Deedee really didn't care diddly why it had all happened in the first place, as long as it vanished.

Goodness, she felt so much better. She was back in control of herself, under her own command.

Everything was fine and dandy.

Chapter Four

The next afternoon, Ryan signed his name to a typed bid for the security system he was recommending to Deedee for Books and Books.

He leaned back in the creaking office chair and laced his fingers behind his head, staring up at the ceiling.

To properly submit a bid from MacAllister Security Systems, he couldn't just drop it in the mail. Although he didn't use terminology to describe the equipment to be used that would be like a foreign language to the average citizen, there were invariably options to consider and more than one type of system available. This created questions that needed to be answered.

It was his policy, therefore, to make an appointment with the prospective client and thoroughly explain the suggested systems, as well as answer any questions that might arise.

It was up to him to take care of that part of the business, as neither his secretary, nor the two installers, had any experience in verbally presenting a bid.

Which meant, he knew, that he had to once again meet with Deedee Hamilton on a one-to-one basis.

Ryan got to his feet and went to the window, looking out over the parking lot that fronted the row of small, single-story offices in the complex. He folded his arms across his chest and frowned, not really seeing what was within his view.

The current situation with Deedee was disturbing and ridiculous. He was an ex-cop who had faced danger, even death, on more than one occasion in the past. He was physically strong, mentally alert and had sharp, quick reflexes, all of which had held him in good stead during his years on the police force.

And at this moment, this point in time, he'd rather walk into a dark alley where he knew some thugs were waiting to jump him than open the door to Books and Books and enter that store.

Yeah, really ridiculous.

He shook his head and returned to the chair, his frown deepening.

How was it possible that a woman, who probably didn't weigh more than a hundred and twenty pounds, could have him shaking in his shorts, wanting to put as much distance as he could between them?

Deedee caused him to act and react beyond his own control. His size, strength and police training weren't worth a damn when he was in close proximity to Deedee. She tied him in knots, took up space in his brain, made his body hot and hard with the physical want of her.

Hell, she even had freckles on her nose that were so damn cute he couldn't help but smile when he saw them, and big, brown eyes like a delicate fawn.

Ryan muttered an earthy expletive, then propped his elbows on the worn arms of the chair and made a steeple of his fingers. He narrowed his eyes and concentrated on the problem at hand.

He didn't know why Deedee Hamilton could turn him inside out. It wasn't as though he'd been knocked for a loop by a woman he'd just met. That would be bad enough, because he had no intention of allowing anyone to take Sherry's place. But Deedee? He'd known her for several years. Why was she getting to him *now?*

He'd managed to escape from Books and Books yesterday without talking to her further. She'd been busy with a customer, so he'd left his card on the counter, along with a hastily written note saying he'd be in touch soon with the bid.

He'd hightailed it out of there so fast that an observer might surmise that a dozen pit bulls were nipping at his heels.

Damn it, he had to get a grip on this mess. Deedee wasn't going to disappear into thin air. She was considered a part of the MacAllister clan, and would be in attendance at family gatherings in the future. He needed to figure out what plan of action would result in him regaining control of his responses to Deedee and return things to normal.

"Yes," he said aloud.

Yes...what? What was the plan?

Okay, MacAllister, try this. When he'd been a kid, his mother had limited how much candy her brood could eat. In a rebellious move, he'd spent the money he'd earned from his paper route on a huge stash of candy that he'd hidden—crummy criminal that he'd been—under his pillow. His mother had discovered the illegal bounty the next day when she'd changed the sheets on his bed.

Wise woman that Margaret MacAllister was, she'd calmly informed him that at ten years old it was time for him to make more of his own decisions. He could, therefore, keep the candy and consume it with no interference whatsoever from her.

Puffed up with his newly authorized independence, he'd proceeded to eat the entire bag of candy in one sitting. Several hours later, he was convinced he was dying, he wouldn't live until morning. To say he'd been sick was putting it mildly.

Now then, Ryan thought, he needed to apply the lesson learned by that scenario to the dilemma with Deedee. Instead of trying to keep out of her way, put distance between them, he should do just the opposite. He'd see her, be with her, as much as possible. He'd overdose on Deedee, just as he'd done years before on candy.

"Excellent," he said. "Brilliant."

After surviving his candy binge, he'd realized he'd do very well with the occasional treat his mother provided. Candy once again took its proper place in his life.

The same principle applied to Deedee Hamilton. By sticking to her like Super Glue he'd be able, in a very short time he was convinced, to view her as the friendly, pleasant woman she was, but who had no particular effect on him.

"MacAllister," he said with a rush of relief, "you're such a genius, you're awesome."

Ryan was jolted from his self-congratulatory reverie by the office door suddenly being opened.

Ted Sharpe entered the room. Ryan's former partner on the police force was tall, blond and tanned. Handsome and nicely built, as well, he never lacked for female company.

"Hey," Ryan said, smiling, "how's it going? What are you doing here in your spiffy cop clothes?"

"I just got off duty," Ted said, sinking onto a wooden chair in front of the desk. "There's a flu bug sweeping through the department and we're short on healthy bodies. I pulled a double shift. I'm headed for home and some much-needed sleep. Man, it was nuts out there. The radio was squawking almost continually. That new restaurant by the park got ripped off, by the way."

"No kidding? They get much?"

"Didn't go near the cash drawer. They took a valuable painting off the wall, then split. The owner had hung it there to impress his fancy patrons. What it did was impress some sleaze, and now they have it. All we can do is hope one of the fences who keeps us informed of business on the streets will come through with some information."

"Sounds like the scum are trying for class. You know, showing they have culture, good taste. It's always nice to witness people attempting to improve themselves."

"Cute," Ted said, then paused. "Mel Poley, the guy they hired to take your place when you quit the force, gave thirty days' notice today. He's going over to Denver because he likes to ski. I won't miss him, believe me. As a partner he didn't cut it for me."

"So you've said many times. He's trigger happy."

"In spades. Your old spot will be open again, Ryan. I want you as my partner again, man. Captain Bolstad would hire you back in a New York minute."

"Don't start, Ted," Ryan said wearily. "We've been over this turf a hundred times."

"I haven't said one word about it for at least six months."

Ryan glared at him. "Go for another six."

"Come on, Ryan, at least think about it, will you? I don't care how many times you've told me you're doing fine sitting behind that desk, I still don't believe it. You liked being a cop, and you're a damn good one. You quit in a knee-jerk reaction to what happened to Sherry, but you quit on life back then, too. Things are different for you now."

"Finished?" Ryan said, his jaw tightening slightly.

"Yeah," Ted said, "I suppose." He got to his feet. "I'm outta here, but . . . damn it, MacAllister, you're so stubborn. If you'd be honest with yourself, really honest, you'd admit you miss being a cop. Not only that, we were good together, great partners. We were so in tune that we practically read each other's minds when we came up against something we had to handle. Perfect partners, that's what we were, and now your old spot is opening up. That's fate. It's time for you to come back where you belong."

"Goodbye, Ted."

"Hell." Ted started toward the door, then stopped, half turning to look at Ryan again. "How was the party for the twins?"

"Fine, great. Those cop teddy bears you got them were a hit with the dynamic duo."

"I should buy *you* one and tape it to your desk. You'd realize soon enough that you belong in one of those uniforms, too."

"Lighten up, Ted," Ryan said, a warning tone now evident in his voice.

"Yeah, yeah."

"Are you busy tomorrow night?" Ryan asked. "The whole clan is meeting for pizza in connection with The Baby Bet Forrest has going about Jillian."

Ryan related The Baby Bet details, and Ted whooped with laughter.

"Forrest is dead meat," Ted said. "Three girls? Even if twins *do* run in your family, triplets are a whole new ball game, predicting in the big leagues. Ole Forrest is about to lose The Baby Bet for the first time, and you'd better believe I'll be at Mario's to witness it. Are you going?"

Ryan shrugged. "Thought I would."

"Really? That surprises me."

"It surprises *me,* but what the hell, why not? We can watch Forrest eat crow while we have pizza."

"Yep. Well, I'm off to get some sleep. I'll see you tomorrow night. Think about what I said before, Ryan. You and I could be partners again, just like it used to be. See ya."

"Yeah," Ryan said quietly as Ted left the room. "See ya."

Ryan continued to stare at the open doorway. *Just like it used to be,* Ryan's mind echoed. Nothing would ever be like it used to be. When Sherry had been killed, his whole life had fallen apart, lost purpose and meaning.

So, yeah, Ted was right when he'd said Ryan had resigned from the force in a knee-jerk reaction to Sherry's violent death. He'd admitted that to himself many months ago. He hadn't wanted to be a cop anymore after the nightmare that had happened. He hadn't wanted *anything* but to be left alone.

Ryan glanced around the small, sparsely furnished office.

MacAllister Security Systems was doing all right. He was getting new customers all the time and was establishing a reputation for top-of-the-line installations. He never attempted to sell someone more than they needed in order to accomplish what they were after, and he guaranteed his work.

Yes, his fledgling company was prospering.

And as the days passed into weeks, then months, he was becoming more and more bored. The challenge of starting a business from scratch had probably saved his sanity at the time he'd done it. He owed his family and Ted a helluva lot for hauling him out of his alcohol-induced haze and trashed apartment when they did.

But now? There was a flat-line sameness to each day, nothing that made him eager to get out of bed in the morning and come to the office.

He picked up a pencil and rolled it back and forth between his palms, staring at it absently.

Ted was his best friend, knew him better than his own family did. They'd spent a lot of hours together in that patrol car over the years and had talked about all and everything. Each knew he would risk his life for the other, and that fact took friendship to a depth that ordinary men didn't experience on a daily basis.

Yes, Ted Sharpe knew him very well. Ted Sharpe knew that his buddy, Ryan MacAllister, was stagnating in an office. Ted Sharpe knew that Ryan wanted to be a police officer again so badly he could taste it.

Ryan snapped the pencil in two, then flung the pieces into the metal wastebasket next to the desk.

"Satisfied, Sharpe?" he said aloud to no one. "I admitted it. Okay?"

He sank back in the chair and dragged his hands down his face.

So? he asked himself. Why wasn't he on the telephone to Captain Bolstad? Why wasn't he saying to the man in charge that he wanted to apply for his former position as Ted's partner on the force?

Because he was scared.

Because he broke out in a cold sweat just thinking about it.

He wasn't afraid of the physical danger that went along with putting on the uniform and gun. Facing possible injury or death wasn't what held him in an iron fist, kept him captive in that shabby little office.

It was the fear of caring.

It was the fear of awakening emotions that he had shut down, put into a hibernating sleep.

A good cop—and he was a damn good cop—had to *care* about the people who cried for help, who needed his expertise, who were counting on him to make everything all right. Each time he responded to a call, he put not just his body on the line, but his emotions, as well. That was what it took to be the kind of cop that he and Ted were.

He had cared deeply in the past, not only as a police officer, but as a man. He had loved. *Sherry.* When she had died, he'd felt as though he were slowly bleeding to death, his life's purpose leaving him drop by painful drop.

If he opened those doors again, tore down the protective walls by rejoining the police force, the ramifications would go far beyond when he was just wearing the uniform.

There would be no halfway measures he could take. If he allowed himself to once again be vulnerable as a cop, it would encompass his entire being, the part of him that was simply a man, as well.

No!

He couldn't, wouldn't, do it.

He had no intention of ever again stripping himself bare, having no defenses. *Not ever.*

Deedee Hamilton was, for some unknown reason, triggering physical reactions in him that he'd been certain he'd put into cold storage with his emotions. But he had formulated a plan to defuse Deedee's unsettling impact on him. The basic principle of overkill was going to remedy that nagging nuisance of a situation in short order.

With a decisive nod, Ryan flipped open a file on his desk. He then spent the next ten minutes rummaging through his desk in search of a new pencil.

The next morning, Ryan was at Books and Books ten minutes after Deedee opened the store. She was standing behind the counter, sipping coffee from a ceramic mug, which she set down in order to greet Ryan.

"Good morning," she said, smiling.

There went her heart again, she realized, suddenly beating in a rapid tempo as though she'd just jogged a mile. Well, fine, let it go nuts. She had her reactions to Ryan all figured out. She must remember the theory of the common cold having to run its course. My, my, wouldn't Mr. MacAllister pitch a fit if he knew she'd categorized him along with a germ?

"How are you this morning, Ryan?"

Totally in control, Ms. Cute Freckles on Your Nose, Ryan thought smugly.

"I'm very well, thank you," he said, then placed a dark blue folder on the counter. "I have the bid you wanted for the security system. You can study it, then get back to me with any questions you might have. Or we can go over it together now. Which would you prefer to..." His voice trailed off as his glance fell on the coffee mug. "Where did you get that?"

"Get what?" she said, totally confused.

"That mug."

She picked it up and held it at eye level. "Isn't it pretty? I bought it at that new gift shop that opened down the block."

Ryan frowned as he looked at her. "It has butterflies on it." Just like in the dream, that damnable dream.

"Well, um, yes, I noticed that myself. I think butterflies are lovely. You know, delicate and beautiful, especially considering they started out as caterpillars. I think that whole process is rather magical." She paused, then put the mug back on the counter. "Ryan, is there a reasonable reason why you're glaring at my coffee mug, or are you just basically strange?"

"What?" He snapped his head up to meet her eyes again. "Oh. I wasn't glaring at it, I was studying it because it's attractive. Yes, that's what I was doing. It's a great mug, very nice."

"Whatever. Would you like some coffee?"

"No, thank you. What do you prefer to do about the bid?"

"I'll look it over now, if you have the time. Why don't you browse through the store while I'm reading this? Then if I have any questions we can tackle them while you're still here."

"Okay. Sure. I'll just look around."

Deedee watched as Ryan wandered off, admiring his physique shown to perfection in dark slacks and a pale blue dress shirt open at the neck.

My stars, she mused wistfully, *that man truly does have a marvelous tush.*

In the next instant she blinked, picked up the file folder and told herself to behave.

Ryan flipped absently through a book he'd taken from a shelf, not really seeing what he was looking at.

Butterflies on Deedee's coffee mug, he fumed. He'd come across like an idiot when he'd seen those butterflies, but they had blindsided him, caught him totally off-guard.

Lord, that was eerie. He'd dreamed about Deedee being captivated by beautiful butterflies, only to discover that she actually was enchanted by them enough to have bought that mug.

And then there had been that woman who had come into the store and asked for a book about butterflies at the exact same time he was standing there.

Very eerie.

Deedee Hamilton was a witch, a spell weaver, a...

MacAllister, knock it off, he admonished himself. Deedee was *not* a witch. She was a woman. She was an especially pretty woman this morning in a soft pink sweater and navy blue slacks. He liked her hair, the way the curls fluffed around her head and cheeks. And that nose. That nose with the cute-as-a-button freckles got to him every time.

Yeah, he could feel it, the coiled heat low in his body. Deedee had pushed his sexual buttons again, right on cue. So be it. He had a plan of action to put an end to this nonsense. Deedee Hamilton's days of turning him inside out were numbered, by damn.

Fifteen minutes later, Ryan went back to the counter. Deedee had assisted two customers during his wait, but had now closed the file and given it a pat.

"You write a very clear and understandable report, Ryan," she said pleasantly. "I expected this bid to be so full of technical jargon I wouldn't be able to grasp it at all."

He shrugged. "I could have written it that way, but it serves no purpose, because I'd have to turn right around and explain it in layman terms. This is more efficient in the long run."

"How did you know enough about this type of equipment to open a security systems company right after leaving the police force?"

"We study security systems at the police academy, so I knew the basics. Then I borrowed a stack of textbooks from a buddy of mine who teaches this stuff in a trade school. I crammed for several weeks. Once I investigated who the best suppliers were, I was ready to go. Now I'm on mailing lists that provide me with the information on the new systems being produced. It's not all that tough."

"Well, *I'm* impressed. It must be challenging to come into a home or business and decide what is needed."

No, he thought dryly, it was boring as hell, to *him*, anyway. But he wasn't about to divulge *that* news flash to Deedee.

"Challenging." He nodded. "Yep."

"I think I understand what you're recommending. The cabinets with the rare books will be on a silent alarm connected to the police department. The wiring will be dropped behind the walls so it won't be unsightly, and I'll press a button hidden under the counter to activate it when I leave, and turn it off when I arrive."

"Right. Or you can have a numbered code activator, which is safer, but more expensive. The sheet is there on that one, too. I recommend the code type because you're running the risk of a thief finding the hidden button and—bingo—he's home free. The chances of him getting lucky and hitting your code are about as good as winning the lottery. In other words... zip."

Deedee nodded, a thoughtful expression on her face. "I see. I want my rare books protected, Ryan. Dealing in these editions had been a dream of mine for a long time. I can remember having lunch with Jillian the day the first cabinet with the wired glass was being built. I was so excited I could hardly sit still."

She swept one arm through the air.

"Now? I have four cabinets and over two hundred rare books. If anything happened to them, I'd be devastated. I want the coded system, Ryan. There's no doubt about it in my mind."

"All right. Just sign those papers accepting the bid, and I'll order the supplies."

"Will I be able to add to the system in the future as my inventory increases and I have more cabinets built?"

"Good question, and the answer is yes."

"Wonderful," she said, smiling.

"It's a pleasure to see someone enthused about what they're doing with their life," Ryan said quietly. "Your eyes are sparkling and... Well, I'm happy for you that you get such a rush from what you do."

Deedee's smile faded and she cocked her head slightly to one side.

"Don't *you*, Ryan? What I mean is, you *did* say that you found your work challenging."

"Well, let me put it this way. There are jobs, and there are careers. What you have here at Books and Books is a career. MacAllister Security Systems is my job."

"I understand," Deedee said softly, looking directly into his eyes, "and I'm sorry. You should have *more*, you *deserve* more."

Damn it, Ryan fumed, unable to tear his gaze from Deedee's. Why had he said that, revealed something so deep and personal? She was doing it to him again, this spell weaver of a woman, making him act out of character.

He was in worse shape than he'd thought in regard to the effect Deedee Hamilton had on him.

He shifted his eyes to the folder, then pulled a pen from his shirt pocket. He handed the pen to Deedee, while looking at her chin.

"If you'll sign that, I'll get out of your way. After I talk to the supplier and check the job schedule at the office, I'll give you a call and let you know when we can start.

"You can be thinking about whether you want the work done during regular business hours, or after you've closed. There's drilling to do, which is noisy and creates dust, which you might feel is too disruptive to your customers who like to take their time in here."

"Not only that," Deedee said, pointing one finger in the air, "there's also the fact that if a would-be crook comes in while you're working, he'll be able to see exactly what you're installing. He might not be able to figure out the code, but he could determine a way to cut the wires inside the walls."

Ryan chuckled. "It's a thought, but I think you read too many mysteries."

Darn him, Deedee thought. She really wished he wouldn't make that sexy sound. It created instant desire that swirled within her, thrumming low and hot.

"Well, Deedee," Ryan said, "whatever you want is fine with me."

Deedee's eyes widened as she had the irrational thought that he'd read her mind.

"What?" she said.

"If you want the work done after-hours, that's when we'll do it."

"Oh. Yes." She cleared her throat. "I'll give it serious consideration and let you know." She signed the paper. "There you are."

Ryan picked up the folder and accepted his pen that she extended toward him.

Do it, MacAllister, he told himself. *Put your plan into action.*

"Listen," he said, "are you still going to Mario's tonight for pizza, and to witness Forrest's defeat as the champion of The Baby Bet?"

"Yes. I'm looking forward to it. It should be a fun evening."

"Why don't I pick you up and we'll go together? That will be one less vehicle trying to park in Mario's lot, which isn't all that big."

Not a chance, mister, Deedee thought. One of the stipulations she'd made to herself while Ryan was running the course of the common cold was that she mustn't be alone with him. Having him there in the store didn't count, because people kept popping in and out. But allow him to pick her up at her apartment and go with him—alone—to Mario's and back? Not in this lifetime.

Ryan took one of his business cards from his shirt pocket and set it on the counter.

"I know which complex you live in because Andrea pointed it out to me once, but why don't you write your apartment and phone number on the back of that?"

"Oh, well, I don't think—"

He interrupted her, his voice very low, very rumbly and very, *very* mesmerizing.

"Six-thirty, Deedee. That should give us plenty of time. All right?"

"Yes," Deedee heard herself say.

Chapter Five

Deedee flicked a brush through her curls, then her hand stilled as she glared at her reflection in the bathroom mirror.

She was so angry with herself, she was beyond having any kind of rational inner dialogue. She just fussed and fumed, and called herself uncomplimentary names for allowing herself to be in the predicament she was in.

Per the usual routine, one of her part-time employees had arrived at Books and Books at five-thirty to take charge of the store until closing at eight o'clock.

Deedee had driven home, taken a lilac-scented bubble bath, then dressed in jeans, a chocolate brown sweater and tennis shoes.

Her hand had hovered over the padded hanger holding a lovely peach-colored sweater with lace inserts, the action causing her to purse her lips in self-disgust.

She'd joined the MacAllisters for pizza before and knew they came to Mario's in very casual clothes. The peach sweater was meant to be worn to a fancy outing, not to a rustic pizza parlor. The fact that the image of Ryan had flitted into her mental vision as she'd hesitated over the peach creation did nothing to improve her mood.

That the brown sweater she'd chosen to wear was the exact shade of her eyes was coincidence she was hereby ignoring, having dismissed it as unimportant.

Deedee smacked the light switch in the bathroom and marched into the living room, where she plunked down on the sofa.

Oh, that Ryan MacAllister was a slick son of a gun, she thought, narrowing her eyes. He knew, lady-killer that he was, that suddenly speaking in that low, sexy voice made women putty in his hands. He no doubt had practiced aloud until he'd perfected the rich, rumbly sound, then laughed himself silly every time it worked on some unsuspecting woman.

What she couldn't fathom was why he had done it. His entire family was going to go nosy-nuts when she and Ryan showed up together at the restaurant.

Andrea had nearly raced across the room to get to Deedee at the twins' birthday party after Ryan had left, all because Ryan had smiled, for Pete's sake. Simply smiled!

That Ryan had suddenly pushed some kind of emotional button and changed back into who he had been before Sherry's death was a ridiculous thought. The walls around him were solidly in place, and even if he chose—which Deedee didn't believe—to emerge from behind them, it would take time and effort to accomplish that goal.

No, the real Ryan was still closed and aloof. The tricky Ryan, who was due to arrive in ten minutes, was up to no good. He was trying to accomplish something, was using her as a pawn to do it, and she was rip-roaring mad.

Deedee tapped one fingertip against her chin.

She was not one to play games and was always honest with the men she dated. But, by gum, Ryan was playing some kind of game with *her* and he was definitely *not* going to get away with it.

So, yes, she'd succumbed to that diabolical voice he'd whipped on her, but she now saw it for the farce that it was. He was probably overflowing with nauseating smugness as he drove to her apartment at that very moment.

There wasn't time to even begin to attempt to figure out why Ryan had insisted they go to Mario's together. Male minds were such messes it often took hours to decipher the whys and wherefores of what men said and did. That puzzle solving would have to go on hold.

"However," Deedee said, getting to her feet, "I *can* give as good as I get."

Ryan had started this game-playing fiasco, and she intended to finish it. The cocky, arrogant side of Mr. MacAllister that had surfaced in her store was in for a shock when he got to her apartment.

A knock sounded at the door and Deedee spun around.

"You asked for it, bub," she muttered, then crossed the room.

Flinging open the door, she immediately stepped back and swept one arm through the air.

"Come in, Ryan," she said. Jeans and a black sweater. Nice, very nice. Oh, who cared? She was furious with this man, and he was about to get his comeuppance.

She closed the door and turned to face him.

"Good evening, Deedee," Ryan said pleasantly. "Are you ready to—"

"Oh, my, yes," she said. "I certainly am."

She moved forward, slid her arms around his neck, molded her body to his and kissed him.

Ryan stiffened and his eyes widened in shock at Deedee's unexpected actions. But in the next instant, heated desire exploded within him, consuming him. He wrapped his arms around her slender body, parted her lips and returned her kiss in total abandon.

He was lost, swept away by passion's rush as he savored her taste, her flowery aroma, the exquisite feel of her body pressed to his.

Yes! his mind thundered. Oh, yes, he wanted this woman. He wanted to make love with Deedee Hamilton now. *Right now!*

Dear heaven, Deedee thought hazily, *this kiss is ecstasy.*

This kiss should never end.

This kiss was something she'd been waiting for for a very long time without even realizing it.

This kiss had been a terrible mistake!

With every ounce of willpower she could muster, she tore her mouth from Ryan's, then wiggled out of his embrace. She took two steps backwards and wrapped her hands around her elbows as she drew a deep, steadying breath.

Ryan blinked, shook his head slightly, then frowned.

"I assume..." he started, then cleared his throat, "there's a reasonable explanation for your behavior, Ms. Hamilton?"

Damn, he thought, she was beautiful. The sweater she was wearing was the exact color of her incredible brown eyes. He ached for her, wanted her with an intensity he could not remember experiencing before. His plan of overkill had been a good one. It had been well thought out. But she'd blown his program to smithereens.

And he was mad as hell.

"Well?" he said. "What do you have to say for yourself?"

That did it.

Deedee was thoroughly shaken by her total response to Ryan's kiss, by the desire still thrumming low in her body. She felt out of control, vulnerable, and she hated that truth. Mentally scrambling for a safe hold, something to grab on to, she found her anger beneath the smoldering passion.

"*My* behavior?" she said, none too quietly. She splayed one hand on her chest. "Mine? Oh, look who's talking. It doesn't sit too well when the tables are turned, does it, Mr. Macho?"

Ryan narrowed his eyes and matched her volume. "What in the hell are you talking about?"

"Don't play innocent with me, mister. I fell for your oh-so-sexy voice when you were saying what time you'd pick me up tonight. Score one game-playing point for you, MacAllister. What happened when you walked in here was a dose of your own medicine. *My* point."

"Oh," he said quietly.

"Yes, 'oh.' I don't play games, Ryan MacAllister, but you forced me to by your own actions. Why you wanted us to go to Mario's together, I have no idea, nor do I care. I won't be used. Is that clear?" She lifted her chin. "I'd appreciate it if you'd leave my home."

Ryan looked at her for a long moment before he spoke.

"No," he said finally.

"No?" She pointed to the door. "Go."

"No. I want to apologize for what I did to convince you to go with me tonight. You nailed it—it was calculated and finessed. I must be losing my touch from lack of use, because you're the first woman to figure it out."

"I happen to be extremely intelligent," she said with an indignant little sniff.

"Okay. That's easier to take than my having lost my touch."

"Oh-h-h," she said, rolling her eyes heavenward, "you're despicable. Go away."

"Not until you accept my apology." He paused. "Then I'll accept *your* apology, and we'll have a clean slate again."

"*My* apology? What on earth for?"

"You're yelling again, Deedee."

"Damn straight I am. Why would I apologize to you? You're the one playing games here."

"Which you could have verbally accused me of when I arrived. Your method of addressing the issue was..."

Ryan stopped speaking as memories of the sensuous kiss shared with Deedee slammed against his mind.

"No, forget it," he said. "You don't owe me an apology. That kiss was sensational. I don't care if you did it for revenge or whatever, it was still sensational."

"Yes," Deedee said softly, "it was. It was supposed to be my way of...but then...oh, dear."

Their eyes met, held and neither moved, or hardly breathed. The embers of desire within them still glowed and began to grow hotter, threatening to burst into raging flames.

Ryan jerked his arm up and studied his watch as though it was the most fascinating thing he'd ever seen.

"We'd better hit the road," he said, tapping the watch, "or we'll be conspicuously late getting to Mario's."

"We're going to be conspicuous just arriving together. I think we should go in separate cars."

"We'd still get there at the same time since we're both leaving from here."

"Well," she said, "I'll drive around the block a couple of times at Mario's and wait for you to get inside."

Ryan folded his arms over his chest. "Oh, really? Doesn't that come under the heading of playing games, Ms. Hamilton?"

Deedee sighed. "Yes, I suppose it does. It's just that your family is going to go ballistic when we walk into the restaurant together. You know that's true, Ryan. It will be 'Wow, look at that. Deedee and Ryan are together. Isn't that something? Isn't that super?'

"Then they'll be watching us like hawks, and trying to get each of us alone for all the details. I love your family as though they were my own, but they definitely like to be in on what's happening in everyone's life."

"We'll weather that inquisitive storm. We'll tell them the truth—there's nothing happening between us. Nothing at all."

Right? Ryan asked himself in the next moment. Yes, of course that was right. He'd already figured out that there was a sexual attraction between him and Deedee that was justifiably labeled old-fashioned lust.

The physical want was causing him to think about Deedee a great deal—to have annoying dreams about her and a bunch of butterflies—but his plan of "overdosing on Deedee" would solve all of that.

There weren't any emotions involved in this mess.

But what about that kiss? a nagging little voice in his mind asked him.

The kiss had been . . . yeah, okay, sensational. But that was understandable, because she was the first woman he'd kissed in nearly two years. He'd reacted to the kiss like a thirsty man in need of water. That made perfect sense.

Why he wasn't consumed with guilt for having broken his vow to stay loyal to Sherry, he didn't know. Forget it. He wasn't using up any more mental energy analyzing one simple kiss.

"I repeat," he said, "there's nothing happening between us, and that's what we tell my family if they push for information."

"I don't suppose you'd care to explain to me why you were so determined to get me to go with you tonight?"

"Not really."

"Fine, whatever," Deedee said. "I'll get my purse, and off we go to Mario's."

There is nothing happening between us, her mind echoed as she hurried into the bedroom for her purse. That was absolutely correct. She didn't care diddly if that answer did, or did not, satisfy the MacAllister clan. Facts were facts, and the truth was the truth. *There was nothing happening between her and Ryan.*

And that kiss?

What about that kiss?

Oh, well, it had been . . . it had been . . . sensational, to borrow Ryan's description. But it didn't *mean* anything, other than they kissed sensationally together, or some such idiotic thing.

And that had *not* been disappointment that had caused a cold knot to tighten in her stomach when Ryan had said nothing was happening between them. It had been hunger. She was starving, and more than ready for some dinner.

"Pizza," she said, whizzing back into the living room. "Let's go."

The drive in Ryan's Jeep to Mario's was made in total silence, the occupants of the vehicle each lost in their own muddled thoughts.

In spite of Ryan's bravado plan to deal with his inquisitive family with short, precise answers to any questions they might have, Deedee could actually feel the waves of sudden tension emanating from him when they entered the restaurant.

She looked up at him quickly and had the irrational thought that she'd heard his walls clank firmly into place. She recognized the closed expression on his face, and his brown eyes appeared flat and unreadable.

How nice, she mused dryly. The MacAllister clan

wouldn't get in an excited verbal dither over her arrival with Ryan once they glimpsed his don't-come-near-me demeanor. They'd had plenty of practice at cutting a wide circle around this frowning, aloof Ryan.

The group was seated against the far wall at a long wooden table with benches. Deedee managed a small smile and a wave as she and Ryan wove their way through the tables in their path. The restaurant was nearly full as Mario's had a reputation for producing some of the best pizza in town, and the noise level was high.

"Hello, hello," Andrea said, beaming at the pair as they reached the table.

"'Lo, 'lo," Noel said, banging on the tray of her high chair.

Ryan nodded, but didn't speak.

Coward, Deedee thought crossly. He was in his not-speaking mode now, leaving her to deal with the family, all of whom were looking at them with a great deal of undisguised interest.

"Ryan and I were discussing the recommendations he'd made for my new security system at the store," Deedee said, "so we decided to come on over here together." That wasn't a lie, it was simply the truth stretched a tad.

"Well, it's lovely to see you both," Margaret said. "Do sit down."

Deedee slid gratefully onto the bench, hoping that once she was seated everyone would forget she was there. She landed next to Ted, then Ryan sat next to her, sandwiching her between the two men.

"Hi, Ted," she said, smiling brightly. "How's things in the world of crime?"

Ted matched her smile. "Business is booming...unfortunately. We seem to suddenly be dealing with crooks with culture. A valuable painting was stolen from a restaurant, and last night an antique vase worth a bundle got ripped from a private home. Nothing else was touched. They snatched the vase and split."

"How strange," Deedee said. "You'd think they'd take as much as they could carry."

Ted shrugged. "They seem to know exactly what they're after, get it and leave. The same thing happened at the restaurant when they took the painting. We figure the guys who did the first job did the second one, too."

"Do you have any clues as to who might have—" Deedee started.

"Where are Jillian and Forrest?" Ryan interrupted gruffly. "Forrest organized this get-together."

"They're on their way," Robert MacAllister said. "Forrest phoned and said they needed to make a quick stop, but to go ahead and order. We're getting those pizzas that Jillian introduced us to."

"Ah, yes," Deedee said, smiling. "Super Duper Pizza Supreme Deluxe Extraordinaire. One very delicious pizza. Did Forrest give any hint as to the results of Jillian's ultrasound?"

"No," Robert said, "not a word. I couldn't tell a thing by his voice on the phone, either."

"He's not winning The Baby Bet this time," Andrea said. "He's been the champion for so long that he's getting illusions of grandeur. Triplets. Three baby girls. No way."

"No way," Matt said, throwing a cracker onto the floor.

"You tell 'em, Matt," Andrea said, smiling at the toddler. "Right?"

"Right," Matt echoed. "Right, right, right."

"Deedee," Andrea said, "would you like to go to the ladies' room with me?"

"No, thank you," she said pleasantly. No way, to quote Matt. She wasn't about to be cornered by Andrea, who would grill her unmercifully for more details regarding her arriving with Ryan.

"Nice try, Andrea," Jenny said, laughing, "but no cigar."

"Mmm," Andrea said, wrinkling her nose.

"Jillian and Forrest just came in," Robert said. "Forrest is carrying an enormous shopping bag. The stop they had to make was apparently at that department store."

"Curiouser and curiouser," Michael said. He rubbed his hands together. "I can hardly wait for Forrest to be unchampioned. He's so darn cocky about The Baby Bet."

"With just cause," Ted said. "He always wins."

"Not this time," Michael said.

Jillian and Forrest reached the table and everyone stared at them.

"Sit down, sweet wife," Forrest said, then dropped a quick kiss on her lips.

Jillian sat next to Ryan, a rather bemused expression on her face.

"Get on with it, Forrest," Michael said. "They'll be calling our order number for the pizzas any second now. Admit you lost, then shut up."

"You have an attitude, big brother," Forrest said, smiling. "I trust that I have everyone's undivided attention?"

"Indeed you do, son," Margaret said. "I would suggest, however, that you make your announcement regarding the results of the ultrasound right now, before someone strangles you, dear."

"Oh," Forrest said. "Good point." He shifted the large shopping bag to one arm. "Okay, here we go. The test showed, with no doubt whatsoever..." He reached into the bag and pulled out a pink, stuffed-toy rabbit, which he set on the table.

"A girl," Jenny said. "It's a girl."

Forrest whipped another pink rabbit out of the bag and placed it next to the first.

"*Twin* girls," Margaret said, laughing in delight. "How marvelous."

"Well, now," Robert said, "isn't that wonderful?"

Then to the group's wide-eyed amazement, Forrest took a *third* pink rabbit from the bag!

"Oh, my gosh," Andrea said, her hands flying to her cheeks.

"I don't believe this," Michael said.

"Believe it," Jillian said weakly. "I don't know if I should laugh or cry. I'm numb."

"Still champion of The Baby Bet," Forrest boomed, "is yours truly, ladies and gentlemen. Jillian and I are expecting triplets, three baby girls."

Everyone started talking at once. Margaret got up and came around the table to hug a pale Jillian and a beaming Forrest.

Deedee stared at the pink rabbits.

Three babies, she thought incredulously. Jillian and Forrest were going to have three precious miracles. It was overwhelming and wonderful at the same time. My, my, she was going to be a busy Aunt Deedee.

But not a mother.

She'd play with the triplets, then go home.

Alone.

Tearing her gaze from the toys, her breath caught as she realized she'd unknowingly wrapped her arms around herself beneath her breasts. It was as though she was attempting to erase the emptiness, the fact there was no baby of her own for *her* to nestle in her arms.

What in heaven's name was the matter with her? she wondered frantically. Her decision years ago to never marry again, to not have a husband and children, had been completely thought through.

The choice to devote herself to Books and Books had resulted in fulfillment, contentment and inner peace. She was happy with the life-style she had, she truly was.

Then why, why, why was she feeling so chillingly alone?

Why had Forrest's proud announcement, and the three grinning pink rabbits, caused a cold shiver to consume her, and threatening tears to create an achy sensation in her throat?

As everyone around the table continued to chatter on in excited voices about Jillian and Forrest's news flash, Deedee felt as though she had floated outside of herself, was hovering above the group like a ghostly observer. She was suddenly separate and apart; she no longer fit there, no longer belonged there, among the joyful family.

She was alone.

"Deedee?" Ryan said quietly. "Are you all right?"

She blinked and shook her head slightly as Ryan's voice brought her back into herself with a jarring thud.

"What?" She turned her head to meet his gaze, seeing the genuine concern on his face and in his eyes—those brown eyes that now radiated warmth and caring. "Yes, of course. I'm fine. I'm just so...so surprised about the triplets. My goodness, Forrest won The Baby Bet again, didn't he? Isn't that something?"

"Yeah," Ryan said, studying her face. "He's still the champion. Three baby girls. Man, Jillian and Forrest are going to be very busy."

"And very blessed," Deedee said softly.

"They're calling our order number for the pizzas," Michael said, getting to his feet. "Come on, Forrest, you can help tote them. You should pay for them, too, since you won all The Baby Bet money again.''

Two waitresses appeared with pitchers of soft drinks and a stack of plates. A flurry of activity commenced with everyone preparing for the pizzas to arrive at the table.

Ryan looked at the pink rabbits again and frowned.

He didn't care how "fine" Deedee claimed she was, he thought, it wasn't true. She was white as a sheet, and he was certain she was very close to bursting into tears.

Why?

Hell, he *knew* why. He wasn't an ex-cop for nothing. He recognized clues and evidence when they were right in front of him.

Deedee Hamilton wanted a baby.

Chapter Six

The drive *back* to Deedee's apartment was as silent as the drive *going* to the restaurant.

Deedee stared out the side window. She was drained, emotionally and physically exhausted and was very cognizant of the fact that she was both confused and angry.

The confusion plaguing her now pushed the muddle over her sensual reactions to Ryan to the back burner. Up close, and disturbingly personal, was the strange and frightening chill of emptiness and loneliness that had consumed her as she'd looked at the three pink rabbits.

She'd been unable to shake off the unsettling emotions, and had forced a false facade of cheerfulness through the remaining hours of the family gathering.

At least she could find solace in the fact that no one had been aware of her inner turmoil.

That she'd been hurled into her gloomy state of mind by three pink toy rabbits was ridiculous. Yes, all right, the rabbits represented babies, were symbols of what she would never have. But that was due to *her* choices, *her* decisions regarding her existence, her future, what she wanted from life.

And, thus, came the anger, which was directed solely at herself for her asinine behavior.

What she needed, she decided, was to put an end to this day, get a good night's sleep and greet tomorrow fresh. She'd then be back to normal, doing fine.

Deedee slid a glance at Ryan.

It was still early evening, she mused, and the expected socially acceptable thing to do would be to invite Ryan in for coffee and chitchat.

Under the circumstances, that was *not* a good idea. The dilemma regarding *him* wasn't going to stay tucked away for long, and she certainly didn't have the mental energy to deal with it tonight.

She would thank him politely at her door for the taxi service to Mario's, bid him adieu, then scramble under the blankets of her bed and not emerge for five years. Well, at least not surface until her alarm went off the next morning. Excellent idea.

Ryan pulled into the lot edging Deedee's apartment complex and parked. He turned off the ignition, unsnapped the seat belt, then got out of the Jeep and came around to assist Deedee from the vehicle. They entered the building without having spoken.

Thank you for the ride. Good-night, Deedee mentally practiced as they approached her door.

"Your key?" Ryan said when they stopped.

"Oh, well, I can..." Deedee started.

"Humor me," he said, holding out one hand. "I'm old-fashioned."

Deedee retrieved the key from her purse and dropped it into Ryan's palm. As he turned to insert the key in the lock, she began her rehearsed speech.

"Thank you for the—"

"Do you have any coffee?" he said, opening the door. He stepped back and extended one arm. "After you."

Deedee entered the living room with Ryan right behind her. He closed the door, clicked the lock into place and gave her the key.

"Coffee?" he repeated, raising his eyebrows.

Deedee mentally threw up her hands in defeat. She couldn't tell him to hit the road without being extremely rude. Coffee. Fine. But this was going to be the fastest cup of coffee ever consumed.

"I'll make a pot," she said, snapping on more lights, then placing her purse on a chair. "Sit down, Ryan. I won't be long."

She hurried across the room and into the small kitchen beyond. As she pulled the coffeemaker forward on the counter, she realized that Ryan was standing next to her.

"I'll bring it into the living room," she said, glancing at him.

He leaned back against the counter, folded his arms over his chest and frowned.

"I'm fine right here," he said.

Deedee shrugged and busied herself preparing the coffee.

Ryan watched her with narrowed eyes.

MacAllister, he ordered himself, *keep your mouth shut.* He'd argued with himself during the drive back here, reaching the conclusion that he had no intention of addressing Deedee's reaction to the dumb pink rabbits.

It was none of his business. So what if he'd witnessed her upset, had seen as clearly as a flashing neon sign the message that she yearned to have a baby of her own? It didn't matter one iota to *him.* He had no desire to learn the inner workings of Deedee's mind, or the secret wishes in her heart.

He had intended to say good-night to her at the door, but had suddenly heard himself request a cup of coffee. Well, that was understandable. He'd been raised to be polite, and since it was still so early, it would have appeared rude to just dump Deedee off and split.

So, fine. He'd drink his cup of coffee...fast, talk about something mundane like the weather, or a current best-selling novel, and be out of there.

Good plan. No problem.

"Deedee," he said, "since you want a baby so badly, why don't you get married and have one? Or don't get married and have one, anyway?"

What? his mind thundered.

"What?" she said, holding two mugs in midair.

"Oh, hell," he said, dragging his hands down his face. "I wonder if early dementia runs in my family."

Deedee plunked the mugs onto the counter, planted her hands on her hips and glowered at him.

"I don't recall saying I wanted a baby, Mr. Mac-Allister, but even if I did, which I don't, it certainly wouldn't be any concern of yours. A baby? Me? That's absurd."

"The hell it is," he said none too quietly. "I was sitting next to you all evening, remember? I saw your reaction to Forrest's rabbits, to the announcement that Jillian is expecting triplets.

"The smile you plastered on your pretty face for the rest of the evening was as phony as a three-dollar bill. Not only that, you were so pale your freckles looked like spots on a dalmatian. Oh, yes, Ms. Hamilton, you definitely want a baby."

"You've got a lot of nerve, mister," she said. "You have no idea what you're talking about, and I really resent your—"

"Ah, Deedee," he interrupted quietly, a gentle tone to his voice. He cradled her face in his large hands. "Talk to me. Trust me."

It was too much, it really was.

If Ryan had continued to shout, Deedee could have held on, matching him holler for holler. But this? The gentle coaxing of his voice, the warmth of his chocolate brown eyes, the comforting feel of his hands on her cheeks, was her undoing.

She was so exhausted, so confused and frightened, and Ryan was a safe haven, a tower of strength, a chance to lean, just for a moment.

She looked directly into the dark pools of his eyes and burst into tears.

"Oh, man," Ryan said, "now I've done it."

He dropped his hands from her face, wrapped his arms around her and nestled her close. Deedee circled his waist with her arms, laid her head on his chest and wept.

And Ryan held her.

He dipped his head and savored her delicate aroma of lilacs, then rested his rugged cheek on her silky curls, allowing them to caress his skin like soft velvet. Her slender body was pressed tightly to his body, her breasts crushed enticingly to the hard wall of his chest.

She trembled as she cried, and fierce emotions of protectiveness and possessiveness consumed him, causing him to clench his jaw.

Nothing, and no one, would ever hurt Deedee Hamilton, he mentally decreed. She was so fragile, like a...yes, a butterfly. He would stand between her and harm's way, keep her sheltered from pain.

She was so sad, was crying as though her heart was breaking. Deedee was meant to smile, to dance in the sunshine with the butterflies. If she wanted a baby, she should have her baby, and a special man to love and cherish her as the precious treasure she was.

Ryan frowned and lifted his head.

A man? his mind echoed. A faceless man who would reach for her in the night, make love to her, plant his seed in the feminine darkness of her body? A man who would watch her growing big with his child, then witness the miracle of that baby being born? A man who would place a pink or blue toy rabbit in front of the MacAllister family as part of The Baby Bet?

Damn it, if any man touched Deedee Hamilton, he'd take him apart!

Ryan shook his head slightly, and his frown deepened.

What in the hell was the matter with him? His mind was charging full-speed ahead down a road that led to Deedee being *his,* the baby she yearned for being *his.*

No!

He was married in his heart and soul to Sherry, always would be. He couldn't, wouldn't, ever love another woman. He'd chosen Sherry as his wife, and he intended to stay true to that vow. No one could ever take her place.

It was the tears, he reasoned. Deedee's sad weeping was unraveling him, shredding him into pieces. That was understandable. Unless a guy was made of stone, he was undone by a crying woman.

Even tough cop Ted was jangled by a weeping woman, even a strange one encountered while in his role as a police officer.

Deedee wasn't a stranger, someone Ryan didn't know. She was Deedee, who had been on the fringes of his life for several years. His emotions had momentarily run away from him, but he was getting himself together now, back under control. If Deedee wanted a baby, she should have one, but *he* certainly wasn't going to have anything to do with the conception.

The Baby Bet might very well be put into operation again in the future, featuring Deedee Hamilton, but Ryan MacAllister would place his twenty dollars in Forrest's hand and watch it all unfold from the sidelines.

Deedee sniffled, then stiffened in Ryan's arms, bringing him from his tumbling thoughts.

"Oh, dear," Deedee said, then a wobbly little sob escaped from her lips.

She eased away from Ryan, and he released her. He took a pristine white handkerchief from his back pocket and handed it to her. She dabbed at her nose and eyes, refusing to look at him.

"I'm sorry," she said, staring at the middle of his chest. "I'm so embarrassed. I don't cry." She paused. "Well, I obviously just did, but I usually don't. I can't even remember the last time I cried, it's been so long. I'm very tired, you see, and . . . But that's no excuse, and I do apologize for—"

"Deedee."

"You're very kind, Ryan, and patient, and . . . I'd appreciate it if you'd go now and allow me to be mortified alone. Try to forget this happened. Okay? Oh, you didn't get your coffee. I owe you a cup of coffee. Good night and—"

"Deedee, look at me."

She shook her head, pressing the handkerchief to her nose.

"Look...at...me."

She sighed, dropped her hands to her sides and lifted her head slowly to meet his gaze.

Oh, hell, Ryan thought, smothering a moan. Her beautiful brown eyes were shimmering with tears, making them shine like starlight. Her nose was pink, her cheeks were blotchy, her lips were trembling slightly. Deedee was not a pretty crier. But Deedee was the most enchanting sight he'd ever seen.

He wanted to scoop her up and hold her close, kiss away the salty tears still streaking her face, then capture her lips with his. He wanted to feel her give way to her passion, just as she'd done during the kiss they shared earlier that evening.

And he wanted to make love to her for the remaining hours of the night—slow, sweet, sensuous love, meshing their bodies, becoming one entity. He'd take her away from reality, carry her to a place where she could dance with the beautiful butterflies.

He wanted... *Damn it, MacAllister, knock it off.*

"Come on," he said, "let's go into the living room, sit down and talk. Just for a few minutes. Okay?"

Before Deedee could reply in the negative, Ryan strode from the kitchen.

"Whatever," she muttered, following him.

Ryan waited until Deedee had sat down on the sofa, then settled next to her, shifting slightly so he could look directly at her.

"Deedee," he said quietly, "I'm very sorry that I upset you the way I did. The fact that you want a baby is none of my business. Well, it *wasn't* any of my business, but now it *is* my business, because I'm the one who made you cry."

Deedee glared at him. "You're babbling."

"Yeah, well, a crying woman is a very traumatic experience for a guy. Being big and strong, able to leap tall buildings in a single bound, isn't worth squat when a woman is crying all over your shirtfront. It's a very helpless feeling."

"Oh. Really? I guess I never thought about it from the male point of view. Of course, I don't go around crying every other minute, either."

"Well, forget all that. The subject here is that something very important to you is missing from your life. What I can't understand is why you haven't done something about it. You're an attractive, intelligent woman. A man would be very fortunate to have you for a wife, a life's partner, the mother of his children. Why are you alone, Deedee?"

"Because I choose to be," she said, her voice rising a bit. "I'm having this conversation with you because it seems like the polite thing to do. You *do* have a soggy shirt because of me and my behavior. However, the bottom line is actually what you babbled about. It's really none of your business."

"You *made* it my business, remember? Why do you choose to be alone?"

"You must have been a good cop, Ryan. The poor suspect would confess just to get you out of his face."

"Yep," he said, smiling. "So answer the question."

Deedee sighed and dabbed at her nose again with Ryan's handkerchief.

"I was married to a wonderful man," she said wearily. "Jim and I were perfect together, absolutely perfect. When he was killed flying an air force jet in a training mission, I was devastated. I hardly functioned for an entire year. I went through the motions of living, but I was actually only existing in a cold, empty void."

"I understand," he said, frowning. "I've been down that road."

"I know you have. At some point, a person has to make choices, get on with their life. I decided to dedicate myself to starting Books and Books, making it successful. I've done that, and I'm very fulfilled, very pleased with what I've accomplished."

"But?" he prompted.

"I don't know what happened tonight," she said, throwing up her hands. "I haven't been pining away for a baby. Keeping in touch with myself is something I pride myself on. What made me react the way I did to Jillian and Forrest's announcement about the triplets? I have no idea. I *am* happy with my life just the way it is, Ryan."

He settled back against the sofa, folded his arms over his chest and squinted at the ceiling.

"No, you're not," he said. "Your subconscious was delivering a message to you that your conscious mind was not yet aware of as being a true fact."

"Oh, good Lord," Deedee said, "now I'm dealing with an amateur shrink. Ryan, go home."

"In a minute." He looked at her again. "You had a *perfect* marriage?"

"Yes."

"There wasn't the slightest glitch, not even one small problem?"

"No."

"Bull."

"Damn it, MacAllister, that's enough. I was there with Jim. I know how it was. He's been dead for ten years, and every detail of our life together is still crystal clear in my mind. I had perfection, and I won't settle for less. The way I see it, what Jim and I had doesn't happen twice, it just doesn't.

"As for my reaction tonight about the babies? I'm human. I suppose, as a woman, there's a tiny seed of desire hidden somewhere within me to have a child, and the three pink rabbits nudged it. It was a fleeting moment that is over. Yes, it upset me because it has never happened before, but it's finished, kaput, done. Go home."

"I'm going," he said, not moving. "Look, just because you made a decision to devote your life to your career, doesn't mean you can't change your mind."

"Is that so? All right, Mr. MacAllister, I'll take a long, hard look at my life, on one condition."

"Which is?"

"That *you* do the same thing with *your* life."

Ryan opened his mouth, closed it and tried again.

"What?" he said.

"You heard me. Your entire family is concerned about who you've become since Sherry was killed.

Can all those people be wrong? You made choices, decisions, just as I did.''

"I'm remaining true to the wedding vows I took with Sherry," he said, his voice harsh. "That's the way it is. That's the way it's going to stay."

"Tsk, tsk. One would think one would practice what one preaches. You *can* change your mind regarding your life-style. You owe it to yourself to re-evaluate your life."

"The hell I do!"

"Neither do I. See? We agree. End of story. Good night, Ryan."

"*You're* the one who cried buckets over pink rabbits, not me. *You're* the one who's in trouble here, not me. I'm doing fine, thank you very much."

"Ha! Any man who kisses a woman the way you kissed me isn't doing so almighty fine in his solitude."

"We covered all that. It's basic lust."

"Oh? But what if it isn't, Ryan MacAllister? What if *your* subconscious is rapping you on your thick skull? What if you want a wife—not me, of course—but a special woman you've yet to meet. And what if *you* want a rabbit?"

"You," he said, pointing a finger at her, "are nuts."

"Am I? Fine. We'll each go on living our lives exactly the way we are."

"You can't do that to yourself, Deedee."

"My deal stands. I examine my existence only if you do the same to yours."

Ryan lunged to his feet. "Man, you're a stubborn woman. You're a real pain in the butt, do you know that?"

Deedee stood, then shrugged. "Whatever."

Ryan ran one hand over the back of his neck and shook his head.

"I don't know why I should care one way or another about what you do with your life." He glared at her. "It's because you cried, I suppose. Tears just wipe me out." He paused, then sighed with exasperation. "All right, you win. If I have to do a reality check on my life to get you to do one on yours, so be it."

"You're kidding."

"Nope. Do you stay late at Books and Books on Friday night?"

"No, one of my employees is scheduled to come in to take the evening shift."

"Good. I'll pick you up here at seven, and we'll go to dinner."

"Why?"

"To discuss what we've thought about, and the conclusions we've reached so far. That's how this is going to work."

"Says who?"

"Me, Ms. Hamilton." He gripped her shoulders, hauled her to him and planted a searing kiss on her lips. "Good night, Deedee," he said when he released her.

"But..." Deedee started, pointing one finger in the air.

Before she could speak further, she heard the door close behind an exiting Ryan.

"Well, hell's bells," she said, rolling her eyes heavenward, then went to bed.

Chapter Seven

Ryan was deep in thought while he shaved the next morning, performing the daily ritual by rote.

He replayed the events with Deedee of the night before over and over in his mind, each time becoming more pleased with how things had unfolded.

Yes, sir, he thought smugly, he'd stepped right in and taken charge, had everything headed in the direction *he'd* decided was the proper way to go. He was calling the shots, making the rules.

He now had a legitimate reason to see Deedee on a regular basis, beyond when he'd be installing the new security system at Books and Books. He would do that job himself, of course, rather than assign it to his employees. The work would keep him in close proximity to Deedee.

Then, due to his genius-level plan, he was in a position to see Deedee regularly so they could work on reevaluating their lives.

Ryan rinsed the razor in the running tap water, then continued to shave.

Deedee was quick on the uptake, he had to admit. She'd nailed him tit for tat, demanded that *he* examine his existence while she was doing hers. That had thrown him for a second, but he'd regrouped fast enough. He'd dish out some malarkey that would satisfy her, prove he was "doing his thing."

In the meantime, he would be accomplishing his goal of "overdosing on Deedee," so he could get her out of his system. He would have the opportunity to allow his sexual attraction to her to run its course, dim, then finally fade out completely.

"Yep," he said to his reflection.

As for Deedee...well, he truly believed that she *did* need to examine her present life-style and be totally honest with herself about what she wanted and needed to be fulfilled and happy.

But why was he pushing her to do that?

So okay, it was time he emerged from his cocoon...a little. Not a lot, just a tad. He fully intended to stay faithful to the vows he'd taken with Sherry, and he wasn't sticking his neck out emotionally in new arenas. He wouldn't render himself vulnerable by again becoming a cop who cared, or by opening emotional doors for a woman to walk through. No way.

He'd loved. He'd lost.

The memories of Sherry would hold him in good stead for the rest of his life. He didn't need more than that, not now, not ever.

He wasn't the one who had cried about pink rabbits, for Pete's sake.

Man, oh, man, he was slick. He'd maneuvered things around Deedee last night like a master chess player.

"You're awesome, MacAllister," he said. "Ow! Damn it, I cut myself."

As Deedee drove to Books and Books, she drummed her fingertips on the steering wheel in time to a peppy tune playing on the car radio.

She felt marvelous, her solid night's sleep having replenished both her physical and emotional energies. It was a new day, the sun was shining and she was in an upbeat frame of mind. It was really amazing what a little rest could do for a person.

Her agreeing to reevaluate her life only if Ryan did the same had been brilliant, absolutely brilliant. Where the entire MacAllister family had failed in their attempts to convince Ryan that he needed to move forward with his life, she was going to succeed.

She was totally confident that Ryan, a basically intelligent man, would come to see that existing behind his solid walls deprived him of a full and rich existence. He'd start to live again, embracing life the way it should be.

As for her? Well, no problem. Her crying jag over the pink rabbits had been a momentary lapse of purpose, a thoroughly feminine and explainable event. It was over, wouldn't happen again and all was well.

Ryan believed she wanted a baby, possibly a husband, but she knew better. She'd have to fake her reports to him on the subject matter to keep *him* on *his* examining track. She wouldn't be lying exactly, she'd be using whatever strategy was necessary to help Ryan. Very good.

"Next up on the agenda," she said aloud.

Her sexual attraction to Ryan had been placed on the back burner, but had to be addressed. It was there, front-row center again.

Oh, dear heaven, when he kissed her she melted, when he touched her she dissolved. The man was potent, dangerous, hazardous to her mental health.

But now she knew that.

She had facts that would enable her to maintain control of her very unsettling passion when she was with Ryan. She'd panicked at first from her reactions to him, but she was under control now, doing fine. What continually happened between her and Ryan was a chemical thing, was . . . lust—nothing more.

Oh, boy, would Ryan be fuming if he realized she was in charge of the present scenario. She would get him to make needed changes in his life, and he'd never know what hit him.

Men might be physically stronger than women, but engage in mental shenanigans? They didn't stand a chance.

"Oh, yes," Deedee said cheerfully, "it's a beautiful day."

* * *

Friday evening, Deedee stood in front of her closet, thoughtfully tapping one fingertip against her chin. She was wrapped in a towel, having just finished showering and washing her hair.

What should she wear for her date with Ryan? He'd simply said they'd go out to dinner, giving no clue as to what type of restaurant he had in mind.

Actually, this wasn't a date, as in *date*. This was a meeting, scheduled so they could discuss the progress made reevaluating their individual lives.

So what did a person wear to a meeting date? Another question to ponder was what in the heck was she going to discuss?

Ryan would pitch a holy fit if she said her plans for the future were centered on increasing her inventory of rare books. Not good, not good at all. He'd want to hear an admission that she yearned for a husband and a pink rabbit. Well, forget *that*.

"I'll wing it," she said aloud. "But what should I wear?"

If they went the fast-food route, it called for jeans and a sport top. A family restaurant meant slacks and a sweater. If they were going to "dine," then a fancy dress was in order.

"Well, darn," she said, frowning, "how can I dress so I'll be prepared for anything?"

Okay, she'd split the difference. She'd wear the peach-colored sweater with the lacy inserts, winter-white slacks, and medium heels.

The last time she wore the peach sweater on a date, she'd added a full-length black skirt and had been dressed to the nines. The outfit she'd just mentally assembled would be halfway between superfancy and very laid-back.

Forty-five minutes later, her hair dried and brushed into soft curls and makeup applied, she looked smashing, if she did say so herself. All she needed was a couple of spritzes of cologne, and she'd be ready to go.

The flowery cologne applied, she turned off the bedroom light and went into the living room, humming softly.

A few minutes later, a knock sounded at the door and she went to answer it, the smile on her face genuine. When she opened the door, the smile slid right off her chin as she stared at Ryan.

Merciful saints, her mind thundered, Ryan Mac-Allister was absolutely gorgeous.

He was wearing a charcoal gray suit with a navy blue shirt and gray tie. A navy silk handkerchief peeked above his jacket pocket. The rich colors did marvelous things, sinful things, for his tan, and his shoulders looked a block wide.

"Hello, Deedee," Ryan said, not smiling. "May I come in?"

Deedee blinked. "What? Oh. Come in? Of course you may come in. Hello, Ryan, come in."

"You're babbling," he said dryly, moving past her. "Do you have a problem?"

She closed the door and turned to face him, willing her smile back into place.

"No," she said brightly, "I don't have a problem. Nope, not me."

He sure as hell did, Ryan thought with a flash of anger. Deedee looked sensational, exquisite, fantastic, and heat had rocketed through his body the moment she'd opened the door.

That sweater she was wearing was a teaser, by damn. A sweater was supposed to be a sweater, not a peekaboo thing with lace whatevers that gave enticing glimpses of the tantalizing woman beneath. Oh, man, this could very well turn into an extremely long evening.

"Are you ready to go?" he said gruffly.

Deedee frowned. "You don't sound very thrilled about the idea. You look about as pleased as a person might if he was leaving for the dentist's office to have a root canal done."

Ryan started to retort, then changed his mind, taking a deep breath instead. He let it out slowly, ran one hand down his tie and squared his shoulders.

"There," he said, smiling. "That's better. I had a hectic day, lots of tedious details to tend to. I didn't have time to 'chill out,' as the kids say, before I came over here. I'm perfectly fine now." *Bull!* "So if you'll get your purse, we'll be on our way."

"Right," she said, eyeing him warily.

The restaurant was a step above "family outing" and a step below "waiters in tuxedos."

She'd dressed appropriately, Deedee decided when they'd been seated.

They ordered from menus offering a wide variety, then Ryan selected, tasted and approved the wine.

"Now then," he said, "we discussed the weather during the drive over here, as well as the royal family of England. Let's get to the nitty-gritty, shall we?"

"Certainly."

Several long seconds ticked by as they looked at each other expectantly.

"Well?" Ryan finally said. "What's your report, Deedee? How far have you gotten in reevaluating your life?"

"Me? Oh, I think you should go first, Ryan. After all, this is your plan, your idea."

"No, I—"

"I insist." She smiled, propped her elbows on the table and folded her hands beneath her chin. "I'm all ears."

No, he thought dismally, she was all woman, and he was a dying man. The drive from Deedee's apartment to the restaurant had been pure agony. Her flowery perfume, the lilting sound of her laughter, the very essence of her femininity, had seemed to fill the interior of the vehicle to overflowing. His body had declared war against his common sense.

Oh, man, how he wanted to make love with Deedee Hamilton.

"Ryan?"

"Hmm?" he said, a rather vague expression on his face.

She leaned slightly toward him. "Are you with me here? What do you have to report?"

"Your salads," the waiter said, suddenly appearing. "Would you care for ground pepper?"

After the waiter had moved away, Deedee picked up her fork and took a bite of crisp lettuce.

"Did you see the size of that pepper grinder?" Ryan said. "The thing must have been three feet long. I should tell that guy that I'm a cop, and he has twenty-four hours to register it as a lethal weapon."

"Well, my goodness," Deedee said, "that is a very interesting observation."

"I beg your pardon?"

"You want to be a police officer again."

"I didn't say..." he said, much too loudly. He glanced quickly around, then lowered the volume of his voice. "I didn't say I wanted to be a cop again."

"Ryan, Ryan, Ryan," Deedee said, shaking her head, "you amaze me. You're the one who is so big on your subconscious sending messages that your conscious mind might not yet be aware of as being facts. That *does* apply to you, too, you know."

"So?"

"So you didn't say you used to be a cop, you said, 'I should tell that guy that I'm a cop.' Present tense, as in now. Therefore—" she pointed her fork at him "—you're saying that you've discovered you want to rejoin the police force. I think that's wonderful. Everyone says you were a terrific cop. Will you and Ted be able to be partners again?"

Ryan sank back in his chair and stared at Deedee as though she'd just grown an extra nose. She smiled at him pleasantly, then took another bite of salad.

Somehow, he thought, narrowing his eyes, Deedee had gained the upper hand here, was calling the shots. How had she managed to do that? Lord, women were difficult to deal with.

The really rotten part of all this was that she was right. He *did* want to be a cop again. He had no intention of pursuing that desire, but a part of him honestly did want to.

Damn it, what was he going to say? He was a MacAllister, and MacAllisters had been raised to tell the truth. They did *not* tell bold-faced lies.

"Ryan?"

He moved forward again, pushed his salad plate to one side and crossed his arms on the top of the table.

"You're quick, Deedee Hamilton," he said. "You'd be a good cop yourself."

"Thank you, sir."

"Let's get something straight here. Whatever we tell each other is to be held in strict confidence and goes no further than the two of us. Agreed?"

Deedee nodded. "Agreed."

Ryan drummed the fingers of one hand on the tabletop, attempting and failing to discover a way to *not* address the issue of his wanting, or not wanting, to rejoin the police force.

"Hell," he muttered.

"Ryan, you're stalling."

He straightened and folded his arms on his chest.

"You're right," he said, "I *am* stalling. I'm not accustomed to talking about myself, what is, or isn't, on my mind. This isn't that easy to do."

"Ryan," Deedee said gently, "in the past two years you've hardly talked at all. You closed down, shut yourself away behind very solid walls."

"Yeah, I suppose I did."

"It's true, and you know it. Believe me, I understand and can thoroughly relate to it. I did the same for the year following my husband's death. But there comes a time when you have to move forward. I think, I hope, you're beginning to realize that."

"How long were you married, Deedee?"

"About eighteen months." She paused. "Jim was on temporary duty in Germany for six months of that, but I wasn't allowed to go with him because it wasn't a permanent assignment. Later he was overseas again for four months, but I never knew exactly where or why. He was an expert pilot, with top-secret security clearance."

"Whew. The air force really took a chunk out of your time together. Had you known him long before you were married?"

"Three weeks," she said, smiling. "We had a classic case of love at first sight. It actually does happen to people."

"Now wait a minute. You knew him for three weeks, were married approximately eighteen months, and he was away for a total of ten months of that year and a half?"

"Yes," she said, obviously confused by Ryan's verbal tally.

He leaned forward again, resting his arms on the table, a deep frown on his face.

"Deedee, for cripe sake, you're refusing to even consider marrying again because you had the 'perfect' marriage? You and Jim weren't together enough to find out more than that you had great sex. I assume you two were sexually compatible?"

"Yes, we were," she said, feeling a warm flush of embarrassment on her cheeks, "but that's not a topic I care to discuss, thank you. What exactly is your point?"

"My point is, when you and your Jim managed to have the opportunity to live under the same roof, the little stuff probably didn't matter because you were never certain when he'd have to leave again."

"What kind of *little stuff?*" she said, a slight edge to her voice.

"Did he pick up his socks? Squeeze the toothpaste in the middle of the tube? Leave a wet towel on the bathroom floor after his shower? Did he help you with the household chores? Take out the trash? Did he remember your birthday? Anniversary? Was he romantic, thoughtful? Did he listen to you, really listen, when you had something on your mind that was important to you?"

"Ryan, that's enough," Deedee said, her eyes flashing with anger. "I'm not going to sit here and allow you to diminish what I had with my husband.

You're picking it apart like...like dissecting a frog, or something.''

"I'm spelling it out in realistic terms, instead of looking at it as the *perfect* fairy-tale romance and marriage the way you are. Add ten years since it all took place, and any rough edges there might have been have definitely been smoothed over.

"Based on this...memory, you've sentenced yourself to a life alone? Deedee, come on, wake up here. You're hiding in a fantasy.''

"Ryan MacAllister, you have no right to pass judgment on—''

"Excuse me,'' the waiter said. "Your dinners.''

"What?'' Ryan said, snapping his head around to look at the man. "Oh, yes, of course. Fine.''

Deedee busied herself by moving her salad plate out of the way, smoothing her napkin—which was already smooth—on her lap, then taking a sip of wine. What she did *not* do, was look at Ryan.

How dare he pass such harsh censure on her marriage to Jim? she fumed. Ryan was being cruel and cold. It was as though he wouldn't rest until he'd shattered her beautiful and precious memories into a million pieces.

Not only that, but he was insinuating—no, it was worse than that—he was stating in no uncertain terms that she was *hiding* in a world of fantasy that she'd constructed with rose-colored memories of her marriage.

That wasn't true. It...was...not...true. What she'd shared with Jim *had* been perfect.

It had been very understandable that he hadn't helped with the household chores. His daily routine was so much more exhausting and stressful than her clerical job at the library.

And the time he'd totally forgotten it was her birthday? Well, he'd explained that. He'd had a rookie pilot with the jitters, who had needed some one-on-one man talk and encouragement. She and Jim had celebrated her birthday on another night.

Hadn't they?

Surely they had, but why couldn't she remember what they'd done together to make it special?

Damn Ryan. For two cents she'd punch him smack-dab in the nose. They hadn't even been discussing *her*. She had zeroed in on his slip of the tongue regarding his *being* a police officer, rather than having *been* one. She thought she had control of the direction of the conversation.

But Ryan had somehow, the sneaky beast, turned things around and begun hammering at her about her marriage. How had he managed to do that? It probably stemmed from the training he'd had in interrogation. All that was missing was a bare light bulb hanging above her head.

Oh-h-h, he was infuriating.

Deedee took a nibble of flaky fish, not really tasting it.

Calm down, she told herself. Regroup. Get it together. She *had* agreed to reconsider her life. That her existence was fine and dandy exactly as it was now was not a declaration she could stand on a chair and holler at the top of her lungs.

If she did, Ryan would no doubt declare *his* life to be in order, as well, and cancel the whole exercise. Not good. *His* life was nothing more than a shallow existence.

So okay, she'd have to grin and bear Ryan's scrutiny of her life so she could have equal time to push him to look closely at his.

Brother, whose dumb idea had this been?

Except...

She really did wish she could remember if she and Jim had actually celebrated her neglected birthday.

"Deedee," Ryan said quietly.

She looked up at him. "Yes?"

"I'm sorry if I upset you. I came on pretty strong, I guess. It's just that I truly believe that you should be embracing life, have more than you do. You should be..." He stopped speaking, searching his mind for the words he wanted. "You should be dancing with butterflies."

Deedee blinked, then drew what she realized was a trembling breath. A warmth suffused her, swept through her like rich brandy, then tiptoed around her heart with a gentle caress.

"That," she said, her voice unsteady, "was one of the most beautiful things anyone has ever said to me."

"Yeah, well," he said, shifting in his chair a bit as he was hit with a wave of embarrassment, "I don't usually say gushy things like that." But that dream was still haunting him, damn it. "But you need to take a hard look at your marriage, as well as your present existence. Do you understand what I mean?"

Deedee nodded. "I think so."

"Good, that's very good. You have a lot of things to sift and sort through before we get together again."

"Yes, I certainly do." She paused. "Ryan, we *were* discussing your wanting to rejoin the police force."

"True. You pointed out that my saying I *am* a cop, rather than I *was* a cop was a message from my subconscious. I need some time to think about that."

"Oh, well, that makes sense. You have your assignment, so to speak, just as I do. You need to concentrate on that topic until we meet again. Right?"

"Right. Now, we've covered the serious business for tonight, so we can relax and enjoy the rest of the evening." He smiled. "Would you care for some more wine, ma'am?"

Chapter Eight

The brain, Deedee mused an hour later, was a strange blob of gray matter. From the moment Ryan had declared they should now relax and enjoy the evening, she'd begun to do exactly that.

There was, she supposed, the possibility that she'd grabbed hold of his statement like a lifeline, only too happy to escape from the overload of thoughts that were tumbling in a tangled maze in her mind.

She did *not* want to examine her marriage to Jim, or her present and future existence, under a mental microscope. She was going to spend the remainder of the evening in the *now,* savoring each moment, one tick at a time.

Ryan was charming, witty and attentive, and the conversation flowed easily from one interesting topic

FREE BOOKS!

FREE GIFT!

PLAY THE "LUCKY 7" SLOT MACHINE GAME!

AND YOU CAN GET FREE BOOKS **PLUS** A FREE GIFT!

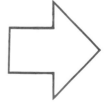

NO COST! NO OBLIGATION TO BUY!
NO PURCHASE NECESSARY!

PLAY "LUCKY 7"
AND GET FIVE FREE GIFTS!

HOW TO PLAY:

1. With a coin, carefully scratch off the silver box at the right. Then check the claim chart to see what we have for you—FREE BOOKS and a gift—ALL YOURS! ALL FREE!

2. Send back this card and you'll receive brand-new Silhouette Special Edition® novels. These books have a cover price of $3.99 each, but they are yours to keep absolutely free.

3. There's no catch. You're under no obligation to buy anything. We charge nothing—ZERO—for your first shipment. And you don't have to make any minimum number of purchases—not even one!

4. The fact is thousands of readers enjoy receiving books by mail from the Silhouette Reader Service™ months before they're available in stores. They like the convenience of home delivery and they love our discount prices!

5. We hope that after receiving your free books you'll want to remain a subscriber. But the choice is yours—to continue or cancel, anytime at all! So why not take us up on our invitation, with no risk of any kind. You'll be glad you did!

© 1990 HARLEQUIN ENTERPRISES LIMITED

This beautiful porcelain box is topped with a lovely bouquet of porcelain flowers, perfect for holding rings, pins or other precious trinkets — and is yours absolutely free when you accept our no risk offer!

PLAY "LUCKY 7"

**Just scratch off the silver box with a coin.
Then check below to see the gifts you get.**

YES! I have scratched off the silver box. Please send me all the gifts for which I qualify. I understand I am under no obligation to purchase any books, as explained on the back and on the opposite page.

235 CIS AX5X
(U-SIL-SE-02/96)

NAME

ADDRESS   APT.

CITY   STATE   ZIP

 WORTH FOUR FREE BOOKS PLUS A FREE PORCELAIN TRINKET BOX

WORTH THREE FREE BOOKS

 WORTH TWO FREE BOOKS

 WORTH ONE FREE BOOK

DETACH AND MAIL CARD TODAY

Offer limited to one per household and not valid to current Silhouette Special Edition® subscribers. All orders subject to approval.
© 1990 HARLEQUIN ENTERPRISES LIMITED   PRINTED IN U.S.A.

THE SILHOUETTE READER SERVICE™: HERE'S HOW IT WORKS

Accepting free books places you under no obligation to buy anything. You may keep the books and gift and return the shipping statement marked "cancel". If you do not cancel, about a month later we'll send you 6 additional novels, and bill you just $3.12 each plus 25¢ delivery and applicable sales tax, if any.* That's the complete price, and—compared to cover prices of $3.99 each—quite a bargain! You may cancel at any time, but if you choose to continue, every month we'll send you 6 more books, which you may either purchase at the discount price…or return at our expense and cancel your subscription.

*Terms and prices subject to change without notice. Sales tax applicable in N.Y.

If offer card is missing, write to: Silhouette Reader Service, 3010 Walden Ave., P.O. Box 1867, Buffalo, NY 14269-1867

BUSINESS REPLY MAIL
FIRST CLASS MAIL   PERMIT NO. 717   BUFFALO, NY

POSTAGE WILL BE PAID BY ADDRESSEE

SILHOUETTE READER SERVICE
3010 WALDEN AVE
PO BOX 1867
BUFFALO NY 14240-9952

NO POSTAGE
NECESSARY
IF MAILED
IN THE
UNITED STATES

to the next as they finished their dinners. They topped off the delicious meal with coffee and small snifters of rich brandy.

"More coffee?" the waiter said, appearing at their table.

Ryan looked at Deedee questioningly.

"No, thank you," she said, smiling. "I'll pop a seam if I have anything more. Everything was excellent, very delicious."

"May I have the check, please?" Ryan said.

"Certainly, sir," the man said. "There's a combo playing in the Malibu Ballroom down the hall if you'd care to dance this evening. I'll bring you the check." He hurried away.

"Well, how do you vote?" Ryan said. "Would you like to go dancing, Deedee?"

"Oh, my, it's been so long since I've danced." She paused. "Let's see, it must be a dozen or fifteen years. Do you suppose it's something that you don't forget, like riding a bike? Well, if I trample your toes, we'll know the answer to that one."

"Twelve or fifteen years?" Ryan repeated. "Didn't you and your husband ever go dancing?"

Deedee refolded her napkin in a precise square, giving the task her full attention.

"No," she said, smoothing the corners of the linen. "No, we didn't." She looked at Ryan again. "Did you and Sherry go dancing often?"

Ryan frowned. "No. Now that I think about it, I realize that I never danced with Sherry." He smiled. "I have a feeling it may be *your* toes that are at risk here. Are you game?"

Deedee matched his smile. "Sure. If we both hobble home, we'll have no one to blame but ourselves."

The waiter returned with a leather folder, which he placed by Ryan. While Ryan settled the bill, Deedee's mind wandered.

She'd never danced with Jim, she thought, and Ryan had never danced with Sherry. Therefore, Deedee Hamilton dancing with Ryan MacAllister was an event, a memory in the making, that was exclusively theirs with no ghosts from the past hovering around. She liked that.

You should be dancing with butterflies.

Ryan's words echoed in her mind, and the warmth she'd felt tiptoeing around her heart when he'd said them returned with greater intensity.

Dancing with butterflies.

Oh, what a beautiful image that created. She could see herself on a sunny summer day, the sky a brilliant blue, and she was wearing a pretty dress. She was... yes, in a field of gorgeous, fragrant wildflowers, and a multitude of delicate, vibrantly colored butterflies were fluttering around her. Ryan was there, and they were smiling.

They were happy and carefree.

They were together.

"All set?" Ryan said.

Deedee jerked at the sudden sound of his voice, instantly aware of the flush of embarrassment on her cheeks for having indulged in such a whimsical and ridiculous daydream.

"You're blushing," Ryan said.

"It's the brandy," she said, pushing back her chair. "Brandy does that to me—makes my cheeks pink. Strange, isn't it? Happens every time."

"Mmm, I see," he said, raising one eyebrow. "Is that a fact?"

"Yep." She smiled brightly.

The Malibu Ballroom was fairly crowded, but Ryan managed to find a free table among those edging the dance floor. Crystal chandeliers had been dimmed to create a romantic glow of soft light. The five-piece band started playing a waltz just as they arrived.

Deedee set her purse on the chair by the minuscule table, and Ryan flipped a plastic sign in a holder to Reserved. They maneuvered their way onto the dance floor, and he drew her into his arms.

As they began to move with the lovely, lilting music, Deedee allowed her lashes to drift slowly down, savoring the moment.

Heavenly, she thought dreamily. Being held fast in Ryan's arms was wonderful. They danced marvelously together, as though they'd been partners on many dance floors in the past.

But, no, there was no past, not tonight. There was no future, not tonight. There was only now, just tonight.

Deedee sighed in contentment and nestled closer to Ryan's powerful body.

Ryan drew a quick, sharp breath as Deedee wiggled against him.

Control, MacAllister, he ordered himself. Dancing had not been one of his brightest ideas. His body was going crazy with Deedee molded to him, the heat within him causing him to ache with the want of her.

Man, she felt sensational, Ryan thought. She fit so perfectly into his arms, against his body, as though she'd been custom-made just for him.

He inhaled her flowery aroma, then dipped his head so her silky curls could whisper against his face. He was going up in flames, but he'd die with a smile.

Deedee felt so delicate, so fragile, so incredibly feminine.

He was dancing with a butterfly.

The waltz ended and the band immediately began to play another slow song. An invisible hand somewhere lowered the glow of the chandeliers another notch. Ryan's hold on Deedee tightened a fraction more.

He attempted to center his mind on the discussion that had taken place with Deedee during dinner, to determine his progress toward getting her to reevaluate her life. He gave up the effort as a lost cause.

He couldn't think, he could only feel.

The hell with it, he decided. He was giving his rational mind the rest of the night off. For the remaining hours he was with Deedee, he wouldn't dwell on the past, or on his loyalty to Sherry. The future, too, would be a taboo subject.

For once in his life, on this night, he was going to simply *be.* He was a man in the company of a lovely and desirable woman. Events would be allowed to unfold with no resistance, no guilt, no ghosts. One stolen night. So be it.

"I guess we remembered how to dance," Deedee said softly.

"Yes, we did," he said, "and we fit together very nicely. You feel good in my arms, Deedee."

"It's nice being here."

They swayed to the dreamy music. The other people on the dance floor seemed to fade into oblivion. There was only the two of them in an otherworld place, where nothing could intrude.

Heated desire swirled within Deedee, pulsing low in her body, and she welcomed it, rejoiced in it. She was so vitally alive. She was woman. This night was special, rare, magical, and hers.

She could feel Ryan's arousal pressing against her, knew he wanted her just as she desired him. The knowledge wasn't frightening, it was wondrous.

"Deedee," Ryan said, his voice low and gritty, "can you feel what you're doing to me?"

"Yes," she whispered.

"I think we should . . . Hell, I *can't* think, I'm beyond thinking. All I know is that I want you, want to make love with you. I ache for you. It's not fair to dump a decision of this magnitude on you, but I have to. It's up to you, Deedee. You're going to have to decide how this night will end."

Deedee tilted her head back to meet his gaze, knowing the raw desire she saw in his expressive brown eyes was evident in her own.

"This night," she said, "is ours. It's a magical night, Ryan, stolen out of time. We're Cinderella and the prince at the ball. One night. Just one. Ours." She drew a trembling breath. "Let's go home...together."

During the drive to Deedee's apartment, she mused rather hazily that if she truly wished at some subconscious level to change her mind about making love with Ryan, the reality of a ride across town in a Jeep would jar her sense of reasoning.

But the fleeting thought was there, then gone. She focused on the moment, adamantly refusing to address anything else.

This was their magical night, hers and Ryan's. Nothing mattered beyond the two of them, and what they were going to share.

Deedee had left a small lamp on in the living room, and the soft glow of light greeted them as they entered the apartment.

When Ryan shut the door, he snapped the lock into place, then quickly shifted in front of Deedee. Startled by his sudden movement, she stepped backward, thudding against the door.

Ryan planted his hands on either side of her head, lowered his own head and kissed her deeply. His tongue plummeted into her mouth and she met it eagerly, dueling, stroking. He kept his body tantalizingly inches away from her.

Deedee curled her hands into fists at her sides, resisting the urge to reach for Ryan and pull him near, to feel his magnificent body pressed to hers.

He lifted his head to draw a ragged breath, then slanted his mouth in the other direction, capturing her lips once again. A quivering whimper of need escaped from Deedee's throat.

The heat grew low within her. It matched the maddening rhythm of Ryan's tongue moving seductively against hers. She was on fire, melting, moist, aching for release and fulfillment.

It was heaven and it was hell, in the same breathless moment.

Unable to restrain herself a second longer, she raised her hands to splay them on the hard wall of Ryan's chest, then lifted them an instant later to encircle his back, silently pleading with him to come closer.

He complied, molding his body to hers, his arousal full and heavy against her. The kiss deepened even more. It was hungry, urgent, fanning the flames of passion even higher and hotter.

Ryan finally tore his mouth from Deedee's, his breathing rough.

"Deedee," he said, his voice sounding strange to his own ears, "I want you. Now. Are you sure, really sure, about this? Have you thought—"

She quieted his words by placing two fingertips on his lips. "I refuse to think about anything other than what I'm feeling, wanting, needing," she said. "We mustn't think, Ryan, either of us. This is our stolen night. There are no yesterdays, no tomorrows, just the now. Make love with me, Ryan, please.''

With a groan that rumbled from low in his chest, he kissed her once more, then swung her up into his arms and carried her into the bedroom. The lamp from the living room cast a nearly ethereal rosy glow over the small room.

He set her on her feet, and she flipped back the spread and blankets on the bed to reveal the sheets. Ryan stared at the bed, his heart thundering so violently it echoed in his ears.

The pattern on the sheets and pillowcases was a multitude of pastel-colored butterflies.

Yes, his mind hammered. Yes. Perfect. There they were, the butterflies from his dream. *This,* what was happening with Deedee, was all a dream. Real but not real. A step apart from the world as he knew it.

Making love was often called the ancient dance of man and woman together. He was about to dance among the butterflies . . . with Deedee.

He looked at her again, then framed her face in his hands. He kissed her softly, tenderly, the whispery caress causing her to tremble. Their eyes met and held. Messages of raging desire were sent and received.

Ryan stepped back and they removed their clothes, allowing the garments to fall to the floor in unheeded disarray.

Then they stood naked before the other, each visually tracing every glorious inch of the one within their view.

Ryan was like a wondrous statue, Deedee mused dreamily. He'd been chiseled from the finest marble by a master craftsman, then bronzed to a warm, rich tone. Each section of his magnificent physique was perfectly proportioned to the next, his muscles ropy, his body powerful.

Brown curls, a shade darker than the sun-lightened hair on his head, covered his broad chest, then narrowed at his belly. A smattering of hair covered his strong legs.

His arousal was a bold declaration of all he would bring to the dark haven of her femininity.

Oh, Ryan.

Ryan drank in the sight of Deedee—her small, firm breasts, the gentle slope of her hips, the nest of strawberry blond curls at the apex of her thighs. She was beautiful, like a delicate china doll, with skin that appeared like ivory velvet.

Deedee.

He lifted a hand, palm up, extending it toward her, not caring that she could see how it trembled. She raised her hand and placed it in his.

It was such a simple gesture, two hands nestled together, one large and callused, the other small and soft.

Two hands. Joined.

It was a symbolic affirmation of the journey they were about to take that would result in the joining of their bodies, meshing them into one entity.

They looked at their hands, but neither spoke, couldn't speak, as emotions flooded through them, unnamed, unknown, but making words impossible.

Ryan tightened his hold, and Deedee stepped forward into his waiting embrace. He kissed her as his hands roamed over her silken skin, cupping her buttocks, lifting, pressing her to the cradle of his hips.

She leaned against him, suddenly weak from the heated flames whipping through her. Ryan raised his head and picked her up, placing her gently among the butterflies in the center of the bed.

Deedee's arms floated upward, welcoming him.

He stretched out next to her, bracing himself on one forearm, his other hand splayed on her flat stomach.

"You're so lovely, Deedee Hamilton," he said hoarsely, looking directly into her smoky brown eyes. "You're beautiful."

"You're beautiful, too, Ryan MacAllister," she whispered. "You truly are."

He kissed her, then moved his lips to one of her breasts, drawing the sweet bounty into his mouth, laving the nipple into a taut button with his tongue. He shifted to the other breast, paying homage there, as well.

Deedee purred in pure womanly pleasure, then the sensuous sound became a near sob of heightening need as Ryan's hand skimmed lower to find the moist curls that shielded her femininity.

Ryan's hand stilled and he lifted his head to look at her.

"Deedee," he said, his voice gritty with passion, "listen to me for a minute. Are you protected, prepared for this?"

"What?" she said, struggling to focus on what he was saying.

"Birth control."

"Oh. Yes. Yes, I'm protected. I haven't been with anyone in such a long time, but I'm on the pill because my body doesn't regulate things too well on its own. It's all right, Ryan."

He dropped a quick kiss on her lips.

"Thank goodness," he said. "If I had to stop now, I'd probably blow a circuit. I want you so much."

"I want you, too, Ryan. I truly do. Now. Please, Ryan, you're driving me out of my mind."

"I don't want to hurt you. You're so small and delicate."

"I won't break. Ryan, please just shut up and—"

"Do it," he said, chuckling. "Your wish is my pleasurable command."

He kissed her once more, then shifted over her and entered her.

"Oh-h-h, yes," she said with a soft sigh. "Yes."

He began to move, slowly at first, then increasing the tempo. Deedee lifted her hips to bring him deeper within her, matching his rhythm.

It was ecstasy.

It was wild, pounding, glorious.

Deedee clung tightly to Ryan's shoulders, feeling the taut, bunching muscles beneath her hands. The heat within her began to swirl and coil low in her body, building to a wondrous tension that seemed to lift her up and away. She savored each thundering thrust that Ryan made, meeting them beat for beat.

Higher...

Reaching...reaching...

Incredible, Ryan's mind hummed. So good, so good. Deedee was tight and hot around him, drawing him deeper within her, giving him as much as he was giving her. They were fantastic together. Oh...man.

On and on...

Higher and higher...

Then...

"Ryan!"

Deedee was flung into oblivion, and Ryan joined her there an instant later, a moan of pleasure from the exquisite release rumbling in his chest.

"Dancing," he gasped, "with butterflies."

They hovered there for a tick of time.

They hovered there for an eternity.

His last ounce of energy spent, Ryan collapsed against Deedee, his breathing labored.

"Too heavy," he mumbled, then rolled off her, keeping her close to his side.

Their breathing quieted, and heartbeats returned to normal. Ryan reached down for the blankets, covered them, then sank back onto the pillow with a sigh of sated contentment.

"Oh, my," Deedee said, nestling her head on his chest. "Oh, Ryan."

"I know. You're right. Unbelievable."

"Yes. Mmm, I'm so sleepy."

He kissed her on the forehead.

"Then sleep, little butterfly."

"Butterfly?"

"Never mind," he said.

Deedee drifted off into blissful slumber, and a few minutes later Ryan closed his eyes and slept.

Hours later, Deedee stirred and slowly opened her eyes. She glanced at the clock, saw that it was 3:14 a.m., then turned her head to look at Ryan. She frowned at the empty expanse of bed next to her.

Maybe he was getting a drink of water, she mused sleepily.

She fluffed the pillow, wiggled into a more comfortable position, then closed her eyes again, allowing thoughts to float in at will.

Ryan. Their lovemaking had been so beautiful. She couldn't remember having ever experienced such ecstasy, such fulfillment.

It was as though she and Ryan had been created just for each other, were *meant* to mesh their bodies, be one, like two perfectly matched pieces of a magical puzzle.

This night had been glorious.

This night? her mind echoed as she opened her eyes again. It was closer to the ever-famous "morning after." Was she sorry, filled with remorse, regret, over what she had done?

No, oh, no. She would cherish the memories, treasure them like precious gifts. The stolen night was hers to keep in her heart, mind and soul.

With morning came reality. Well, so be it. She once again had a past and a future, as well as the now of the present.

The past. Jim. Her darling Jim. Her beloved, who had, indeed, forgotten her birthday, which she now remembered they never did celebrate. She'd cried tears of disappointment and hurt in solitude.

Jim. She had taken second place, always, after the airplanes. His greatest joy came from flying through the heavens, pushing the envelope, taking daring chances and declaring himself to have "the right stuff." Being her husband, lover, friend, had never come first with Jim Hamilton.

She'd loved him so much. She'd forgiven him so much.

And it was time to face the truth.

Her marriage to Jim had not been perfect.

She'd buried the hurt and unhappiness so deeply within her, she'd truly forgotten there had been bad times along with the good. Jim's death had shattered her, caused her to cringe in emotional fear of ever loving again.

Ryan had been right when he'd said she was hiding in a fantasy.

Deedee drew a shuddering breath.

She'd hung on to the past like a lifeline for ten years. *Ten years.* She used it as a shield to keep men at bay, to avoid the risk of loving again.

But on this night, this beautiful night with Ryan MacAllister, the shield had crumbled into dust and was gone. It was time, long overdue, to move forward, grow, embrace the future.

"Goodbye, my darling Jim," she whispered. "Rest in peace, my love."

A warmth suffused her. With it came a soothing sense of inner peace that caused a lovely, soft smile to form on her lips.

A moment later the smile was replaced by a frown as she realized that Ryan had been gone far too long to be simply getting a drink of water.

She left the bed and picked up his shirt from the floor, slipping it on to cover her nakedness. Crossing the room, she stopped in the doorway as she saw Ryan sitting on the sofa in the living room. He was wearing his trousers, had his elbows propped on his knees and his head sunk into his hands.

She started toward him, hesitated, then stopped halfway across the room.

"Oh, God, Sherry," Ryan said, his voice ringing with anguish, "what have I done?"

Chapter Nine

Ryan's words seemed to strike against Deedee like physical blows, causing her to instinctively wrap her arms around her middle in a protective gesture. A chill swept through her, and a gasp escaped from her lips.

Hearing the soft sound, Ryan snapped his head around to look at Deedee. He lunged to his feet in the next moment, pain etched on his rugged features.

"Deedee." He extended one hand toward her, then dropped it back heavily to his side. "You heard," he said, his voice flat and low.

Deedee shifted her arms higher to beneath her breasts, lifted her chin and swallowed past the ache of tears in her throat.

"Yes, I heard," she said, praying her voice was steady. "You've totally destroyed our night together,

Ryan. What we shared. You allowed Sherry's ghost to come into *our* private place, *our* world. You had no right to do that, because this night belonged to me, too. I was the other half of what happened here."

He shook his head. "You don't understand."

Deedee marched across the room to stand in front of him. She planted her hands on her hips and looked directly into his eyes.

"Oh, I understand perfectly, Mr. MacAllister," she said, her cheeks flushed with hurt and anger. "You accused me of hiding in a fantasy of having had a perfect marriage.

"Well, you were right. I did the ever-famous reevaluating of my past, and I admit that I *was* hiding, just as you said. But I'm not hiding any longer, Ryan. I've accepted the truth of my time spent with Jim, the good *and* the bad. *It was not perfect.*"

"Deedee—"

"Shut up and listen. *You're* the one who's hiding now, Ryan. You're scrambling as fast as you can back into the past because you're a coward. You're afraid to hang on to the fact that tonight was incredibly beautiful and rare. So very special. You're afraid, Ryan, actually terrified, that it might come to mean something to you, that you might actually *care.*"

"I broke my vow to Sherry," he yelled. "Where am I supposed to put *that?* What about my personal integrity? How can I look at myself in the mirror when I've been unfaithful to the pledge I made?"

"Sherry is dead!" Deedee shouted. "If she loved you as you claim she did, she'd want you to get on with your life, laugh again, love again, for heaven's sake...live again. Damn you, Ryan, you're hiding, and you're intelligent enough to realize that you are.

"Why? Why are you hiding? Have you asked yourself that question, Ryan? Do you know the answer?"

"Damn straight I do, lady," he said, volume still on high. He dragged both hands through his tousled hair. "I don't want any part of loving again, caring again, not about anyone, or anything.

"I'd like to return to the police force, be a cop. How do you like that news flash? Oh, yeah, I want that very much. I'm bored out of my mind running Mac-Allister Security Systems. But I won't ever wear a uniform again. No way. And I won't ever love another woman other than Sherry. It's not going to happen, Deedee."

"Why not?" she queried.

"Because it's all too risky, damn it. I'm not setting myself up to get sliced in two again. I can't do things half measure, don't you see? If I became a cop, I'd care about the people I came in contact with, all of them. I wouldn't be able to keep myself from doing that. I don't know how. And when I love a woman, I give it everything I have. Everything in my heart and mind. My very soul."

A shudder ripped through him.

"No," he went on, his voice suddenly hushed and raspy with emotion. "I can't do it. I can't run the risk of laying it all on the line, then waiting to have it, the essence of myself, crushed, smashed to smithereens.

A man can only bleed to death once, drop by drop. I've done it. I won't do it again. Not ever.''

"Oh, Ryan."

Deedee's eyes misted with tears, and she closed the short distance between them, wrapping her arms around him and leaning her head on his bare chest. She could feel his muscles tense and the wild beating of his heart, but continued to cling to him.

He slowly, tentatively, lifted his arms to encircle her. His hold was loose, light, just barely touching her. Deedee increased the pressure of her arms. With a moan, he pulled her tightly against him, as though he'd never again let her go.

"Ah, Deedee."

The anguish in Ryan's voice caused fresh tears to brim in Deedee's eyes. Two tears slid slowly and unnoticed down her cheeks.

"Ryan," she whispered, "don't do this to yourself. Don't hide anymore. You deserve to live life to the fullest, to be happy, to have a million special nights like this one we just shared. I don't mean have a relationship with *me,* but you'd find someone special if you'd only break free of the past."

"Deedee, I didn't intend to spoil what we had tonight," he said quietly. "It was truly beautiful. It really was *our* night. We'll keep it separate and apart from everything else. I can do that. I *will* do that. I swear, I promise, I will."

He paused and shifted his hands to her upper arms, easing her back so he could see her face. She lifted her head to meet his gaze, blinking away the last of her tears. He frowned at her.

"What do you mean," he said, "you didn't mean have a relationship with *you?* It sounds as though you're sending me packing to find some woman I haven't even met yet."

Deedee shrugged. "What difference does it make?" She directed her attention to one of the buttons on his shirt she was wearing, pushing it more firmly through the buttonhole. "You've made it clear that you have no intention of having a real present or future. You're staying in the past...with Sherry."

Ryan dropped his hands from her arms and began to pace around the living room with heavy strides. Deedee sank onto the sofa and watched him trek. He finally stopped, folded his arms over his chest and glowered at her.

"You're right," he said. "I'm staying in the past, being true to my vow to Sherry. But suppose, just suppose, I'd decided to let the past go. Why wouldn't you consider having a serious, committed relationship with me? I mean, hell, what am I? Chopped liver?"

Deedee covered her mouth with one hand and coughed to keep from laughing right out loud.

Male egos, she thought, were strange little creatures. Men in total, egos included, were basically weird specimens. Having a relationship with her, or any woman for that matter, was obviously not an option Ryan planned to explore, even consider for a moment.

He certainly didn't want *her* in his life. But her saying she wouldn't have a relationship with him, even if he was available? He was pitching a male-ego fit. Men, men, men. Poor dears, they were such befuddled messes.

A wave of exhaustion suddenly swept through Deedee, and she sighed with fatigue.

It was no wonder she was tired, she thought. It was nearly four in the morning, and she'd dealt with a multitude of intense emotions since the evening with Ryan had begun so many hours before.

"Ryan, look," she said, then yawned. "I need some more sleep. Let's talk about this tomorrow, shall we? I'm out on my feet."

"But..." He paused. "Yeah, you're right. Enough is enough for now. I think the best thing would be for me to leave."

Deedee got to her feet and shuffled slowly toward the bedroom.

"Whatever," she said. "That might be a little tough to do seeing how I'm wearing your shirt, and I'm too pooped to take it off. You could chance it, I guess, and hope you don't bump into anyone you know." She waved one hand breezily in the air. " 'Bye."

"Hey! I need that shirt, Deedee."

"Mmm."

Deedee crawled back into bed, pulled the blankets up to her chin and fell soundly asleep within moments after her head nestled in the soft pillow.

A few minutes later, a muttering Ryan slipped into the bed next to her.

* * *

The aroma of freshly brewed coffee brought Dee-dee slowly awake from a deep, dreamless sleep. She opened one eye to see Ryan sitting on the edge of her side of the bed, holding a mug of coffee in each hand.

"Hello," he said, smiling slightly. "This is room service. I hope you weren't supposed to open Books and Books this morning. It's after nine-thirty."

"No, today is Saturday and one of my employees is working." She stretched, then scooted upward. After arranging the pillows behind her, she reached eagerly for one of the mugs. "Heavenly. I feel very pampered." She took a sip of the hot coffee. "Oh, good grief, this is so strong it could have walked in here on its own."

"I like a robust cup of coffee to get me started in the morning." His gaze flickered over her. "You wrinkled my shirt."

She was sexy as hell in his shirt, Ryan thought, but that was beside the point. The fact that she was surrounded by the butterflies on the pillowcases and sheets and looked pretty as a picture wasn't fair to his libido, either. How could a woman be that beautiful so quickly after awakening?

And there were those damnable cute, polka-dot freckles prancing across her pert nose. No, it wasn't fair at all.

"Well," he said, "leaving in a wrinkled shirt is better than having no shirt at all."

"True." She took another swallow of coffee, wiggled her nose at the bitter taste, then set the mug on the nightstand. "We need to talk, Ryan."

"Now?"

Deedee folded her hands in her lap, resisting the urge to reach out and touch Ryan's enticingly bare chest that seemed to be beckoning to her tingling fingertips.

"Yes, now," she said.

He nodded. "Go for it."

She stared at her hands for a long moment, then met his gaze again.

"I meant what I told you last night," she went on quietly. "I really did take an honest look at my marriage to Jim. I've accepted the fact, *the truth,* that what I shared with him was *not* perfect."

"You were hiding in the fantasy that it was."

"Well, yes, in a way," she said thoughtfully. "But not because I was afraid to love again. I had considered all my choices and made the conscious decision to dedicate my physical and emotional energies to making Books and Books a success.

"The men I dated over the years constantly took the stand that my business was an acceptable entity, no problem. I couldn't get through to them that I didn't want a serious commitment with a man.

"They did, however, head south when they thought they were competing with a ghost, when I said I'd had a perfect marriage that I had no intention of attempting to duplicate. I used it as a tool to end relationships as gently as possible."

"And you came to believe it."

"Yes. I think that's what happened."

"But now? You did react very strongly to Forrest's pink rabbits, Deedee."

She sighed. "I know I did, and that confuses me. I'm still focused on Books and Books, I know I am. I'm enthused, excited, as dedicated to the store's continued success as I ever was. Maybe the pink rabbit episode was a fluke, a blip on my emotional screen that came from a purely womanly part of me. That could happen to any single woman my age. But it came, then it went. End of story."

"Maybe not. Maybe it's the beginning of a new story. Your subconscious could have been sending you a heavy-duty message about what you really want in the future."

Deedee frowned. "I guess I need time to sift through all this." She nodded. "I'm sure I need time.

"Ryan, when I said I wasn't interested in a relationship with you, it wasn't personal. At this point in time, I don't want a relationship with any man."

"That may change after you sift."

She shrugged. "Who knows?"

"Deedee," Ryan said, looking directly into her eyes, "you accused me of being a coward."

"Oh, Ryan, I apologize for that. I had no right to use such a harsh word."

"It's all right, because I can understand why you'd see it that way. I admitted that I was staying in the past because it was too risky not to. That could easily be construed as being a coward.

"However, I view it as being a realist. A person who got creamed standing in the middle of a freeway would be pretty stupid to march right back out into that traffic. He'd stay on the side of the road, where it was safe. That's not cowardice. It's common sense."

"Wrong. I'm not buying your metaphoric scenario. Millions of people have loved and lost, Ryan. That doesn't keep them from loving again once they've worked through their grief."

"Not interested."

"But you've given up being a police officer, too. Darn it, Ryan, why won't you think about all this? You talk about it with a stubborn set of your jaw and a list of what you won't do. I'm the only one working at this 'reevaluation' you invented."

"That's not true. I . . ." He stopped speaking and stared up at the ceiling for a long moment before looking at her again. "Yes, it is."

"Mmm," she said, nodding decisively.

"Okay, it's confession time." He took a deep breath and released it slowly, puffing out his cheeks in the process. "I, um, well, I never intended to seriously reevaluate my life. I said I would because I truly believed that *you* needed to examine your existence." And I needed to overdose on Deedee, get her out of my system, obliterate the strange and unsettling sensual impact she has on me.

As far as that part went, Ryan's progress was zip. His desire to make love with her again was so intense that he ached. He wanted her. *Now.*

"You conned me," Deedee said, frowning.

"I should apologize, I guess, but I won't, because you *did* achieve a realistic picture of your marriage. You've dealt with the past, know the truth, and you're free to move forward with your life. There are still some kinks to work out, but so far you're doing great."

"Kinks?"

"Well, yeah. The pink rabbit episode is unfinished business. All my instincts tell me you sincerely wish you had a baby, and probably a husband, too. You'll cover that when you sift. Are you angry because I tricked you into taking part in this plan?"

"Oh, my, no," she said pleasantly. "I couldn't legitimately be angry at all, because I was doing the exact same thing to you."

Ryan narrowed his eyes. "Oh?"

"Yep. I was perfectly content with my life, but was saddened by your determination to cling to the past, to hide behind the walls you'd built around yourself. Your entire family is deeply concerned about you, Ryan. So I agreed to your little exercise with the condition that you do as much mental homework as you were demanding that I do."

"*You* conned *me*."

"Yes, sir, I certainly did," she said, appearing extremely pleased with herself. "You've made a teeny tiny bit of progress, but nothing to shout about. You've admitted you want to rejoin the police force, but you won't actually do it. You've admitted you're staying in the past because it's safe, but you've convinced yourself that's common sense bordering on brilliance.''

She leaned slightly toward him.

"You have an attitude, MacAllister, that definitely needs work."

"You're pushing me, Deedee," he said, a warning tone to his voice. "I don't like being manipulated, which you did. And I don't like being nagged, which you're doing."

"Matching up to exactly what you did and are doing to me."

"Oh."

"Yes, 'oh.' Well, all the truth cards are on the table, and the question is waiting to be answered."

"Question? Which is?" Ryan asked.

"It's very simple. It's 'now what?' The jig is up, so to speak. Do we cancel the whole thing?"

"No! Damn it, you still have to deal with the pink rabbit."

"And you," Deedee said, poking him in the chest with one fingertip, "have to deal with what you want versus your refusal to go after it."

He snagged her hand with one of his, resting both on his chest.

Oh, blast, Deedee thought. The heat from Ryan's hand was traveling up her arm and across her breasts, causing them to feel heavy, in need of his soothing touch. Heat. It was swirling, thrumming lower in her body, pulsing. She wanted to make love with Ryan *right now*.

She tugged on her hand, but Ryan tightened his hold, refusing to release it.

"Now what?" he repeated. "We continue on with the program."

"Only if we're both honest about it, Ryan. I have to know you're doing your part."

"Yeah, I will, but it's a waste of time, because I'm not going to change my stand."

"We'll see. I study my reaction to Forrest's pink rabbit. You study the possibility of actually moving forward with your life. Agreed?"

He nodded slowly. "Agreed." He paused. "There's another question that needs addressing. What about us?" His gaze flickered over the rumpled bed. "What we shared was fantastic."

"Yes, but you're beating yourself up because it happened."

"No, I've regrouped on that, remember? I said I'd keep our night separate and apart from everything else. I think—no, I'm certain—that I can continue to do exactly that."

Deedee yanked her hand free and folded her arms over her breasts. She glared at Ryan.

"So you can have great sex whenever the mood strikes?" she said. "Not in this lifetime, bub. I don't have casual sex, Ryan MacAllister, and if that's where your head is, count me out.

"Last night was special, rare, wonderful. It meant a lot to me. You're not a stranger off the street— you're someone I know and care about. I don't love you, have no intention of falling in love with you, but I *do* care about you."

"Well, hell, Deedee, if I didn't *care* about you as a person, a woman, a friend, I wouldn't have gone to all the trouble to con you into reevaluating your life."

"You've got a point there."

"You bet I do. To echo...I don't love you, have no intention of falling in love with you, but I do *care* about you."

"You said the word *friend* before."

He nodded. "It applies."

"Friends," she said, squinting at the ceiling, "and lovers. Mmm. It has possibilities." She looked at him again. "Ryan, what if we agreed to be friends and lovers? No commitments to the future, no false declarations of feelings that aren't there.

"The whole evening we spent together was lovely—dinner, dancing, sharing, talking, then...then making love."

"True. Go on."

"Well, we're mature adults. Why can't we set the boundaries as we know them and which match perfectly? Why can't we be friends and lovers? Nothing more."

Ryan thudded his coffee mug onto the nightstand, got to his feet, then began to pace the floor, one hand hooked over the back of his neck.

Damn, this was confusing, he thought. He was supposed to be getting Deedee out of his system, not agreeing to a proposal that would keep her in it.

Friends and lovers. Well, maybe . . . Hell, why not? There was no duplicity going on, everything was up front and honest.

He and Deedee cared enough about each other to make it more than just casual sex. But neither one of them had any intention of falling in love with the other. If a person made up their mind not to fall in love, then they didn't fall in love. It was a matter of having a firm mind-set, and a grip on reality.

It would be nice to have a social life, something to look forward to after a dull, boring day at Mac-Allister Security Systems. And heaven knew that he and Deedee were terrific together in bed.

Friends and lovers.

"Mmm," he said, continuing to pace.

Deedee watched him, her mind whirling.

Friends and lovers? she thought. Was that a bizarre thing to have proposed? Well, no, not really. It made sense, was custom-tailored for her and Ryan. She did *not* want to fall in love and get married again. Her focus was, and would remain, on Books and Books.

And Ryan? Even if he managed to keep what they shared separate and apart from the sifting and sorting he needed to do about his life, surely *some* of the time they spent together would influence his thinking on not staying in the past. He wouldn't fall in love with *her*, nor did she wish him to, but he just might become free enough to eventually love someone else.

Love someone else? Make love to another woman, the way he'd made love to her? Perhaps fall in love, marry and have a child with that woman?

Why did those thoughts cause a cold fist to tighten in her stomach? Why did the image in Deedee's mind of Ryan with another woman cause her to feel empty, lonely, filled with a hollow sense of despair?

Enough, Deedee, she ordered herself. She was still bordering on emotional overload from all that had transpired. She would be happy for Ryan if he found love again, embraced it, married and had a family. Of course, she would. In the meantime they'd be . . .

Friends and lovers.

Yes.

Ryan stopped his trek and looked at her.

"Yes," he said. "It'll work. We'll make it work."

"Oh, well, fine, that's fine." She smiled. "Should we shake hands on it, or something?"

"Or something," he said, starting slowly toward her.

Deedee's eyes widened as she watched him approach, seeing the stark desire suddenly evident in the smoky brown depths of his eyes. A shiver coursed through her, and a sense of tantalizing anticipation. It was quickly followed by the now-familiar heat that thrummed low and hot.

Friends and lovers? her mind echoed. Oh, yes, yes, yes!

Ryan sat down on the edge of the bed and looked directly into Deedee's eyes, seeking and finding an affirmation of what he needed to know.

Deedee wanted him, just as he wanted her. They didn't have to discuss it, he knew, because they made no attempt to hide their desire, their raging passion.

They were so open and honest with each other now, with no more hidden agendas. They'd talked, shared, communicated, and everything was aboveboard and real.

There was no need to feel guilty, to be plagued with remorse for not staying true to his vow to Sherry. What he and Deedee had agreed upon was very different. It was unusual, but suited them both to perfection. It involved only the two of them, excluding all and everything else.

Friends and lovers.

Yeah, it was good.

"I think," he said, his voice low and rumbly, "that I'll reclaim my shirt."

He reached forward and slid the first button free, his fingers caressing Deedee's soft, warm skin beneath the material.

"Do you..." she started, her voice unsteady, "want me to go iron it?"

"No-o-o," he said slowly, "that won't be necessary." One hand moved to cup one of her breasts. She trembled. "What's a few wrinkles between friends?" His thumb stroked the nipple of her breast to a taut bud. "Right?"

"Oh-h-h," she said, closing her eyes for a moment to savor the exquisite sensations rushing through her. "Right. That is... that is so right."

He pulled the shirt free of the sheet and blanket, undid the remaining buttons, then brushed the material back to reveal her breasts to his smoldering gaze.

Planting his hands flat on either side of her hips, he leaned forward, drawing the lush flesh of one breast into his mouth, suckling, flicking the nipple with his tongue.

A soft sigh of pure feminine pleasure whispered from Deedee's lips.

He moved to the other breast, drinking of its sweetness, as one hand skimmed over her hip, down the side of her leg, then came to rest at the apex of her thighs.

"Oh, Ryan, please."

In a blur of motion, he shed his trousers, threw the bedclothes to the foot of the bed, then lifted Deedee from the pillows to lay flat on the field of lovely, pastel butterflies. He covered her with his naked body, claiming her mouth in a searing kiss.

He entered her with one deep, powerful thrust, filling her, consuming her and her senses. She welcomed him, eagerly receiving all that he was bringing to her.

And they danced.

Chapter Ten

Ryan finally left Deedee's apartment, complete with wrinkled shirt covered by his suit jacket. Deedee showered, dressed, nibbled on a piece of toast, then began to clean the apartment, per her usual Saturday routine.

Much to her annoyance, she realized she'd vacuumed the living room, bedroom, then had turned right around and thoroughly vacuumed the living room again.

She smacked the off switch on the vacuum cleaner, then slouched onto the sofa with a sigh.

Flapping one hand in front of her face, she frowned. "Go away, Ryan MacAllister. Get out of my brain. I'm trying to do some housework here."

Ryan, Ryan, Ryan, her mind echoed. Her body was sore in feminine places, but she felt wonderful. She was still acutely aware of every inch of herself, her skin seeming to tingle, her breasts full and womanly.

Oh, such exquisite lovemaking she'd shared with Ryan. She'd never experienced anything so beautiful, complete, anything that had caused her to soar to a wondrous place where she'd never been before, a place where she could only go with Ryan.

He was so strong, yet tempered that strength with infinite gentleness, putting her pleasure before his own. He'd discovered the mysteries of her body, just as she'd done with his, savoring it all.

"Friends and lovers," she said aloud. "Lovers and friends."

Ryan truly *was* her friend. He listened, really listened, when she talked to him. He was concerned about her future happiness, had manipulated her into examining her life out of a sense of caring. She knew, just somehow knew, that if she telephoned him in the middle of the night and said she needed him, he'd come, no questions asked.

Yes, he was her friend.

But he was also very, very dangerous.

It would be extremely easy to fall in love with Ryan MacAllister.

And *that* was not going to happen.

Her existence was constructed exactly the way she wanted it, with her focus on Books and Books. She didn't *really* yearn for her own pink rabbit. She could satisfy her maternal instincts when the urge arose by visiting the ever-growing number of MacAllister babies.

Now she even had a man in her life, a friend, who would provide enjoyable social outings where she wouldn't have to be alert for signs that he was becoming too serious about her or might soon be asking more of her than she was willing to give.

That friend was also her lover, and together they achieved glorious sensual heights beyond her wildest imagination.

"Yes, indeed, everything is perfect," she said, getting to her feet.

Her relationship with Ryan, within the boundaries they'd mutually agreed upon, was exactly right for him, too. He was giving of himself, caring, slowly emerging from behind his protective walls. He would hopefully become free of the past, and eager to move forward with his life.

"Perfect," she repeated, grasping the handle of the vacuum.

She started to wrap the cord around the hooks on the machine, then stopped, staring into space.

If everything was perfection personified, she mused, then why did the apartment seem so incredibly empty? Why was she feeling strangely alone and lonely? Why did she miss Ryan MacAllister so darn much, wish he was still there with her?

"Deedee," she said, "get a grip. You'll see Ryan when you see him. He'll pop up...whenever. Fine."

But, oh, dear heaven, how long would she have to wait before she was able to once again drink in the magnificent sight of Ryan MacAllister?

When Ryan entered his office on Monday morning, he realized that for the first time since he could remember, he was glad to be there. It was not due, however, to a sudden enthusiasm for being the owner of MacAllister Security Systems, and he knew it.

The remainder of Saturday and all day Sunday had dragged by slowly, tediously, causing him to become restless and out of sorts. He'd rejected every idea that came to mind to fill the hours, and the time had hung heavily on his hands.

And it was all Deedee Hamilton's fault!

Ryan sank onto the chair behind his desk and stared moodily at nothing.

Deedee had hovered in his mind's eye the entire weekend. She'd been a haunting, taunting presence, a pest. He'd seen her smile, heard her laughter *and* the womanly purr of pleasure she made when he touched her. He'd actually smelled her delicate, flowery aroma, and vividly recalled the exquisite taste of her velvet-soft skin.

She'd driven him right up the wall, caused him to toss and turn at night as he ached for her, his body hard and hot.

Ryan smacked the top of his desk with the palm of his hand, then swore a blue streak as the pain from the blow shot up his arm.

"Serves you right," Andrea said, coming into his office. "That's what you get for desk abuse." She plopped down in the chair opposite the desk. "A tad grouchy this Monday morning, are we?"

Ryan glared at her. "Don't you have a kid who needs a diaper changed?"

"Nope. The twins are at day-care this morning, tormenting the other two-year-olds. I'm on my way to MacAllister Architects, Incorporated."

"Oh, I see. Well, don't let me keep you. Goodbye, Andrea."

"Tsk, tsk, Ryan. Did you forget this morning to have that muddy junk you call coffee?"

Ryan leaned back in his chair and sighed. "No, I had plenty of my delicious coffee, thank you very much. I'm just exhausted, that's all." He managed a small smile. "Hi, Andrea, how's life? What's new and exciting? How's that? Better?"

"Not much, but I'll take what I can get."

"You haven't come by here in months, little sister. What's on your mind?"

Andrea shrugged. "I just thought I'd say hello. I haven't had you all to myself in ages. What do you think about Jillian and Forrest expecting triplets? Isn't that something?"

Ryan chuckled. "Yeah, it sure is. Man, they are going to be busy beyond belief when those babies arrive. Three of everything. Whew."

"Three girls, just as Forrest predicted. The way he continually wins The Baby Bet is getting eerie. I swear he can't be beat, and he's so darn smug about it."

"He should be. He's on a real roll. He deserves to be cocky as hell with his winning record."

"Yes, I suppose he does." Andrea paused. "So! How's Deedee?"

Ryan raised his eyebrows, an expression of pure innocence on his face. "Who?"

"Don't get cute with me, Ryan MacAllister. A friend of mine—well, actually a friend of my friend—saw you and Deedee out dancing. I think that's wonderful, and I wanted to tell you how pleased I am that you two went on an official date."

"Deedee and I are friends," he said. And lovers. Fantastic lovers. "Read my lips, Andrea. That word is *friends.*"

"That's fine," she said, smiling. "John is my best friend. I'm John's best friend. Being friends is an important part of a meaningful relationship."

"Oh, man," Ryan said, rolling his eyes heavenward, "here we go."

"No," Andrea said, suddenly serious, "I'm not planning to pester you for details about your... whatever it is... with Deedee. I just wanted to say to you, privately, how happy I am that you went out socially. It's a start, Ryan, and it's long overdue."

Ryan looked directly at his sister, seeing the gentle love radiating from her brown eyes that were the exact shade of his.

"Yeah, you're right, it's overdue," he said quietly. "Deedee and I had a nice evening, a good time. We've talked, Andrea, and neither of us wants anything more than friendship."

"I understand." She got to her feet. "I'm glad you discussed it, because I'd hate to see either of you hurt. You're very special people. So you'll enjoy social outings together as friends. That's great. I guess that means you're both free to date other people. Right?"

"I haven't thought about it. Why?"

"Oh, another friend of a friend has an attorney cousin she wants Deedee to meet. I guess this guy is a real hunk of stuff, and has megabucks to boot."

"Whatever," he said, lifting one shoulder in a shrug.

"Then you don't mind if I mention the gorgeous lawyer to Deedee?"

"Andrea, I just said that Deedee and I are only friends. I don't have an exclusive claim on her time. She's free to go out with whomever she pleases. If she wants to date a sleazy lawyer with pumped-up muscles, who throws money around to impress her, that's her choice to make."

Andrea laughed. "You're getting crabby again, and I'm late for work. Forrest probably won't even notice what time I arrive. It's hard to see the clock from up on cloud nine. 'Bye, sweetheart." She blew him a kiss and hurried out of the room.

"'Bye," Ryan said absently.

A megabucks yuppie attorney? his mind echoed. No, that didn't sound like the type of guy Deedee would be interested in going out with. She'd turn him down flat. Wouldn't she?

Hell, he didn't care one way or another. Did he? Definitely not. So fine, she'd go out with the smooth-talking lawyer, who would wine and dine her, bring her flowers, kiss her and . . .

Ryan lunged to his feet.

Kiss her? Touch her? Try to hustle her into bed? He'd tear the creep apart! He'd . . .

"Oh-h-h," he moaned, dragging both hands down his face as he sank back onto his chair. "Deedee Hamilton, you're driving me crazy."

"Hey, boss," a man said, poking his head in the office, "the equipment you needed for that deal at the bookstore just arrived."

"Good. Thanks for telling me."

"You still planning on doing that job, instead of having me and Jack do it?"

"Yeah. Why?"

"Because talking to yourself is a definite sign of old age. I just wondered if you could handle the work."

"Go play in traffic."

The man hooted with laughter and disappeared.

Ryan glowered at the empty doorway for a moment, then shifted his gaze to the telephone.

He needed to call Deedee and inform her that he was ready to install her new security system, and ask her if she wanted it done during the day, or after the store closed. Yep, he had to get in touch with her right away.

He picked up the receiver and began to punch in numbers he vaguely realized he knew by heart.

What Ryan MacAllister *wasn't* aware of was that he was smiling.

* * *

Deedee combed her hair, freshened her lipstick, then practiced three different smiles in the mirror over the sink. In the next moment, she rolled her eyes in self-disgust and left the small bathroom at Books and Books.

Glancing at the clock, she hurried across the room to lock the front door, flipped the sign to Closed, and dropped the bamboo shade into place. She also lowered a shade behind the large front display window.

An automatic timer had turned on several small spotlights to illuminate the arrangements of books in the window, but the shade kept sidewalk browsers from seeing the interior of the store after closing hours.

Ignoring what felt like a full platoon of butterflies in her stomach, she entered the storage room. After flicking on the light, she stood by the back door, waiting for Ryan's arrival.

She was behaving like an adolescent, she admonished herself. This wasn't the captain of the high school football team for heaven's sake, it was Ryan. Her friend. Her... her lover.

She straightened the waistband of her bright red sweater over her black slacks, drew a steadying breath and ordered herself to shape up.

Why was she so nervous? She'd been a wreck ever since Ryan had telephoned to say he was ready to start the installation of her new security system. They'd agreed he'd work after the store closed; he'd see her then, goodbye.

"Fine," she said aloud.

Her jangled state confused her, it truly did. Everything between her and Ryan was under control, up front, honest and open. The structure of their relationship suited them both to perfection, and a dandy time would be had by all.

There was no just cause for her to feel like a kid going to her first prom. Ryan would be there any second now. It was no big deal.

A sharp knock sounded at the back door.

"Oh," she gasped, her hands flying to her cheeks.

Stop it this instant, Deedee Hamilton, she told herself. She had no idea what her ridiculous problem was, but enough was enough. There, she was fine now. Steady as a rock.

She moved closer to the door.

"Who is it?" she said, knowing and hating the fact that her voice had squeaked.

"Ryan" came a muffled reply.

She plastered a smile on her face, then unlocked and opened the door.

Oh, Ryan, her mind hummed. Hello, Ryan Mac-Allister.

"Hi," she said. "Come in." He was gorgeous in jeans and a black sweatshirt. Simply...gorgeous.

"Hello, Deedee." He moved passed her to place a large box on the counter, then turned to look at her. "This is all I'll need tonight. You can close the door. I'll be in and out, so set the lock on open. That will save you from having to perch in here to let me in every other minute. You said you'd be doing paper-work at the counter. Have you eaten dinner?''

Good Lord, he fumed, he sounded like a record stuck on full speed ahead. He'd delivered that non-sensical dissertation so fast it was a wonder he hadn't run out of oxygen and passed out on his face.

What was the matter with him? This was Deedee, his friend, who looked sensational in that red sweater. Deedee, his lover, who was causing heat to rocket through his aching body. *MacAllister, cool it.*

"So you're all set to begin work," Deedee said, a tad too loudly.

"Yeah, I am. Right. Did Andrea talk to you about the lawyer?"

What? his mind hammered. Where had that come from? Just because the attorney jerk had been on his mind was no excuse for the subject to come out of his mouth.

"Lawyer?" Deedee said, obviously confused. "Do I need one? I have one who handles the legal docu-ments for the store but... Am I being sued, or some-thing?"

"No, no, nothing like that." Ryan shook his head and frowned. "Andrea has a friend with a cousin, or brother—hell, I don't know—an attorney with big bucks and matching muscles they want you to meet. Go out with. On a date. Get the picture?"

"I see," she said slowly. "A lawyer."

"A rich lawyer, who pumps iron."

"Mmm," she said, placing one fingertip on her chin.

"So? Are you going to go out with the yuppie, who will probably spend the evening flexing his biceps?"

Deedee dropped her hand from her chin and cocked her head slightly to one side. "Why are you yelling?"

"I'm not yelling!" He paused. "Yes, I am. Forget it. Just forget I mentioned the creep."

She laughed. "He's a creep?"

"Yes. No. How should I know? I've never met the guy. If you want to go out with him, then do it."

"Thank you for your permission, Mr. Mac-Allister," she said dryly.

"I didn't mean to sound like you needed my permission to... Hell, erase this whole conversation. Pretend I just came in. Hello, Deedee."

A warm glow started somewhere low and deep within Deedee and spread like liquid heat through her entire body, creating a flush on her cheeks.

Ryan MacAllister, she thought, did *not* want her to go out with the muscle-bound, rich, creepy lawyer. Wasn't that something? Why that knowledge pleased her so much, she had no idea, but it did. It truly did.

"Ryan, I don't want to go out with the attorney in question."

"You don't?" A smile broke across his face. "That's great. I mean, that's... interesting."

"Well, you see, you and I have set boundaries for our relationship. Should I call it a relationship?" She shrugged. "I guess so. Anyway, I'm comfortable with what we have. Why would I go out with someone who might press me for more than I wish to give?"

"Good point."

"Besides, you and I are lovers. I never date a man if I'm sleeping with another one. It goes against my code of conduct. You, of course, are free to do what suits you in regard to other women."

"I don't want anyone but you." He blinked. "That is, I'm on the same wavelength as you. Our relationship—yeah, we'll call it a relationship—is structured just fine for me. I have no desire whatsoever to enter the singles dating scene. I'll leave that meat market to Ted. So that's settled, then. We don't date other people while we're involved with each other. Agreed?"

"Agreed."

"Good. That's good."

He stepped forward, slipped one hand to the nape of her neck, lowered his head and kissed her.

Her bones were melting, Deedee thought as her lashes drifted down. Oh, dear heaven, she was on fire. It had been an eternity since Ryan had kissed her, but now he *was* kissing her, and it was glorious.

Ryan dropped his hand from her neck and gathered Deedee close to his heated body, pausing only to take a rough breath before claiming her lips again. His tongue delved eagerly into the sweet darkness of her mouth to seek and find her tongue. Deedee splayed her hands on his back, urging him nearer yet.

Yes! Ryan's mind thundered. He'd wanted, *needed,* this kiss like a thirsty man yearning for water on a scorching desert. Ah, Deedee, yes!

He filled his senses with her taste, the familiar aroma of flowers, the exquisite feel of her breasts being crushed against his chest. Memories of the lovemaking he'd shared with her flitted through his mind, increasing his passion to a fever pitch.

His hands skimmed down over the feminine round- ness of her bottom, nestling her to him, his arousal heavy and aching.

Oh, man, how he wanted her.

He would never get enough of her.

For the remaining days and nights of his life, he would savor the ecstasy that was Deedee in his arms— Deedee purring in pleasure as he kissed and caressed every inch of her lissome body; Deedee calling his name as she was flung into oblivion.

Deedee Hamilton was his.

Forever.

Ryan stiffened, breaking the kiss and dragging air into his lungs.

Forever? his mind echoed. No, damn it, he didn't believe in forever, not anymore. Death was the only forever that was absolute, guaranteed. There would be no forever with Deedee.

"Ryan?"

Deedee opened her eyes and looked at him, the de- sire radiating from the smoky brown depths causing him to stifle a moan of matching need.

"I, um..." He cleared his throat. "I have to get to work, Deedee." He eased her slowly away from his aroused, aching body, missing the feel of her the in- stant she was gone.

"Oh, yes, of course." She fiddled with the waist- band of her sweater, willing her skittering heart to re- turn to a normal rhythm. She looked up at him again.

"I'll leave you to it. I have paperwork to do." She hurried out of the room.

Ryan stood statue still, ordering his body back under his command. He told his hazy brain to shift gears, think about electrical wiring. A tug-of-war began in his mind, yanking him back and forth between the intricacies of the security system he was going to install at Books and Books, and Deedee.

And butterflies.

And a cute, freckled nose.

And femininity personified.

And forever.

"No," he said, slamming his hand onto the doorknob.

He started to turn it, then stopped, a deep frown knitting his brows.

There would be no forever with Deedee. That was a given.

But...

When two people had structured a relationship based on the premise of friends and lovers, how long did that arrangement last?

How long would Deedee Hamilton be his?

Chapter Eleven

During the next several weeks, Ryan pushed the haunting, unanswered question to the back of his mind and ignored it. He refused to address the issue of how long Deedee would be his and simply lived each day at a time—each day and each lovemaking night... with Deedee.

Since he was spending his free hours with Deedee, he realized it had been far too long since he'd seen or spoken to Ted. He tracked Ted down, and they agreed to meet at their favorite restaurant for dinner the following evening.

Shortly after six o'clock the next night, Ted slid into the booth in the small café and smiled wearily at Ryan, who sat across from him.

"Howdy, buddy," Ted said. "You are looking at one tired cop. Man, what I wouldn't give to get my hands on those sleazes who are ripping stuff off."

"Which ones?" Ryan said, chuckling. "Or have you cleaned up the city to the point there's only a couple bad guys left?"

"Yeah, right. That won't happen in *my* lifetime. I'm talking about the Culture Creeps. That's what we've dubbed them."

"Ah," Ryan said, nodding, "the guys who take a valuable whatever and nothing else."

"Yep. They've hit two more places. They got an expensive necklace on display in a jewelry store window, and a rare coin from a private home. Can you believe this? Why not clean out the jewelry store? Why leave behind the other coins in the collection? I'm telling you, Ryan, they're driving the whole department nuts. There's no word on the streets. Nothing. Zero. Zip."

"Sounds like they have discerning tastes."

"Culture Creeps," Ted said, then muttered an earthy expletive.

"Have some of Rosie's chili," Ryan said. "It's good for what ails you."

A waitress appeared, the pair greeted her by name, then ordered chili, salad and beer. The woman reappeared quickly with the drinks and a basket of crunchy, warm French bread.

"Rosie saw you two from the kitchen," the waitress said. "She's rushing right now, but said she'd be out to collect a hug from each of you. Oh, yeah, and she said she ought to be smacking you upside the head instead, 'cause it's been so long since you've been here. End of message.''

"Tell her we love her," Ted said. "She's been on our minds day and night all these months."

"Ted Sharpe," the woman said, "you're so full of bull it's a shame. Rosie says you've got the smoothest lines she's heard delivered by any man she's met in her sixty-five years. Oops, your order is up. I'll be right back."

Steaming bowls of chili were placed on the table, along with crisp salads. The two men ate in silence for several minutes, taking the edge off their appetites.

"Rosie hasn't lost her touch," Ted eventually said. "I'm glad you suggested we meet here, Ryan. It's been too long between bowls of Rosie's chili."

"Yeah, it has."

"I was in Books and Books today," Ted went on.

"Oh?"

"Last Christmas my folks gave me a kit for carving a miniature rocking chair. Little tiny bugger. I finally got around to trying it, and it was a complicated son of a gun, very intricate. It turned out halfway decent, if I do say so myself.

"Surprisingly, it's very relaxing work, even though it's precise, and you have to be slow and careful. I bought a book at Deedee's store on making all kinds of miniature stuff."

"There you go," Ryan said. "When you retire from the force, you can be a master miniature maker."

"Yep. Deedee said you installed a security system for her rare-book collection about a month ago."

Ryan nodded and shoveled in another spoonful of the spicy chili.

"I looked at the books through the windows on the cases. She's got some incredible stuff there."

"Yeah, I know. It's an impressive collection, and it's her pride and joy. She enjoys running Books and Books, but get her started talking about those rare books? Man, her eyes sparkle and her cute freckles dance a jig. She got a call the other day from a guy in Paris who wants to buy one of those books. She was so excited, I thought she'd jump right out of her shoes. Then she..."

As a broad smile broke across Ted's face, Ryan frowned.

"Forget it," he said. "What kind of miniature are you going to carve next?"

"Nice dodge, MacAllister, but it didn't work. Why?" Ted held up a finger. "One. Deedee babbled on about you, like you just did about her." Another finger went up. "Two. I bumped into Andrea and she said you and Deedee have been out to dinner with her and John a couple of times, plus you two went to a movie with Forrest and Jillian, and a concert with Michael and Jenny."

"Eat your chili," Ryan said gruffly.

"Three," Ted said, adding the appropriate finger. "You're different."

"What do you mean I'm 'different'?" Ryan glared at Ted.

"*That* expression I recognize, but in the overall you're not tight or wired like you've been the past couple of years. Whatever is going on between you and Deedee Hamilton is good for you, and I'm happy to see it."

"Deedee and I are friends."

"Okay," Ted said, lifting one shoulder in a shrug. "Whatever."

Ryan leaned back in the booth, his hands flat on the table on either side of the large bowl.

"You don't believe me," he said.

"Nope, but that's all right. You'll tell me what you want to tell me when you want to tell me what you want to tell me. I can wait."

"I just told you. Deedee and I are friends."

"Right. No problem." Ted reached for another slice of bread.

"Damn it, Ted," Ryan started, then shook his head.

He picked up his spoon again, stirred the chili left in the bowl, then continued to stir, watching the spoon go around and around.

"Deedee is special," he said quietly. "She's intelligent, fun, sensitive and, Lord knows, she's pretty. She's lovely, in a cute, wholesome way. She's open and honest, no games, no phony-up junk. She's just... Hell, she's just Deedee, herself, real."

"And you're in love with her."

Ryan's head snapped up. "No."

"For God's sake, Ryan, have you listened to yourself when you talk about her? Have you kept in touch with yourself when you're making love with her?"

"I never said we were—"

"Give me a break. I wasn't born this morning. Look, I've never been in love, but I sure as hell recognize it in other people when I see it. You and Deedee are making love, and you and Deedee *are* in love. With each other. You're both down for the count."

"Sharpe," Ryan said, a muscle jumping in his jaw, "go to hell."

"Okay," he said pleasantly. "I sure hope Rosie isn't out of her homemade cherry pie. If she is, I'll arrest her for breach of promise. Do you want that last slice of bread?" He slid out of the booth. "I'm going into the kitchen to give Rosie her hug *and* to see if by any chance there's a cherry pie with my name on it just coming out of the oven."

"Mmm," Ryan acknowledged absently as Ted walked away.

Ted was wrong, dead wrong. He, Ryan Robert MacAllister, was *not* in love with Deedee Hamilton. Hell, *he* knew what love felt like because he'd been in love with Sherry. Ted had admitted to never having been in love. So what made Sharpe think he was such an expert on the subject?

Ryan shoved the bowl forward, then scowled as he folded his arms on top of the table.

So okay, he was a far different man now than the one who had fallen in love with Sherry. He was older and bitterly wiser. And, too, Deedee was Deedee, not to be compared with Sherry.

But love was love.

Right?

He'd been in love before, so he'd sure as hell know if he was in love again.

Wouldn't he?

Or was it unique each time, sort of custom-tailored to who the people were when it happened?

Good Lord, was it possible that he *was* in love with Deedee, but hadn't recognized the emotion for what it actually was?

"No," he muttered, "that's not possible."

Was it?

Ted plunked a plate in front of Ryan, then slid back into the booth with his own plate.

"A hug goes a long way with Rosie," Ted said, rubbing his hands together. "Look at the size of these pieces of pie. Dig in, MacAllister."

"You're crazy," Ryan said, still glowering.

"You don't want to eat Rosie's cherry pie hot from the oven? More fool you, dude. I'll gladly have your slice after I finish mine."

Ryan pulled the plate toward him. "You touch it, I'll break your arm. Your crazy zone is in regard to your saying I'm in love with Deedee. I'm not in love with her. She's not in love with me."

"You can deny it from here to next Tuesday, but it won't change the facts as they stand." Ted took a bite of pie. "Mmm. This is heaven on this mess called earth. How come you're free to have dinner with me tonight?"

"Deedee had a Women in Business meeting," Ryan said, then sampled the dessert. "Yeah, great pie. Rosie never fails."

"So," Ted said, "if Deedee were free tonight you'd be with her?"

Ryan shrugged. "We're together most evenings. Her place, mine, whatever. We eat out, or cook dinner, rent a movie, read, or watch the tube. You know, ordinary spending-the-evening-hours-doing-something stuff."

"Like the millions of married couples across the country."

"Would you knock it off, Sharpe? Change the subject, or I'm out of here."

"Chill, MacAllister. The subject is changed."

"Good."

"Of course that won't keep you from thinking about it. You'll have trouble sleeping tonight, buddy, because you're going to be replaying this conversation over and over in your tiny mind. You'll be tossing and turning, tossing and turning. Guaranteed."

"Sharpe," Ryan said, a definite warning tone to his voice.

"Okay, okay, don't get hostile. I'm changing the subject." He paused to take another big bite of pie, chewed and swallowed. "I'm riding solo on duty these days. Poley went on over to the Denver force."

"Why hasn't Captain Bolstad assigned you a new partner?"

"He's advertised the job, but hasn't clicked with any of the applicants. In fact, the city council increased our budget and Bolstad is looking for three cops. So far, he's got zip."

"Oh," Ryan said, nodding, "I see."

Ted didn't speak further as he finished his pie. He pushed the plate to one side, then leaned back in the booth, sighing with contentment.

"Okay," Ryan said, "get on with it before you blow a circuit."

Ted raised his eyebrows. "Get on with what?"

"The spiel about me rejoining the force. You laid the groundwork with your 'Bolstad is looking for three cops' jazz, so go for it."

"Nope, I've given up on you. I'm just wasting my breath trying to get you to come back. I'll just have to wait and see who Bolstad hires and assigns as my partner."

"Yeah, well, I'd probably have to do the refresher course at the academy because it's been so long since I resigned. He'd surely have the positions filled by then, anyway."

"You didn't resign."

"What?"

"Well, you did, but that's not how the captain put the paperwork through. You're on an official leave of absence, which means you wouldn't have to do the refresher course. You can *unleave* yourself and be back in uniform within forty-eight hours."

"He had no right to do that!"

"Captains can do whatever they damn well please. But you're not interested, so he'll hire three guys as soon as he can find them. Want me to change the subject again?"

Ryan stared at him for a long moment, then chuckled and shook his head.

"You're good, Ted, very slick, very tricky. I believe it's called reverse psychology." Ryan's smile faded. "I'm going nuts running MacAllister Security Systems. I'm bored out of my mind.

"I messed around a couple of days ago, making up a contract that would enable my two installers to buy the outfit from me if they wanted it. I haven't said anything to them about it. I haven't said anything to anyone, not even Deedee, but..." His voice trailed off.

Ted watched him intently, hardly breathing.

"I miss it, Ted," Ryan continued quietly. "I really miss being a cop. I guess the caring, the emotional involvement with the people, is part of the package when you're wearing the uniform. Risks. Hell, life is a risk at every turn. I'm running risks caring about Deedee. I said *caring*, not *loving*, but it's still risky, yet I'm doing it. I think that..."

He stared up at the ceiling and drew a shuddering breath, before looking at Ted again.

"It's time, Ted," he said, his voice slightly husky. "I'm so damn tired of hiding out in that dingy office." He nodded. "Yeah, it's time to put on the uniform and go back to where I belong. Don't say anything to Captain Bolstad until I've told Deedee. She deserves to hear it from me before I actually do it. Then I guess you'll have yourself a partner."

Ted smiled. "Welcome home, buddy."

Ryan matched his smile. "Yeah."

* * *

Hours later, Ryan punched his pillow, gaining momentary satisfaction from pretending it was Ted Sharpe's nose.

Damn that Sharpe, he fumed, rolling onto his back in the rumpled bed. He couldn't sleep because of Ted's power of suggestion at dinner that the night would consist of tossing and turning. Tossing and turning, and thinking about the issue of being, or not being, in love with Deedee Hamilton.

During the short time he *had* slept, he'd had the dream again, the same dream about Deedee dancing with the butterflies.

"Oh, man," Ryan said, dragging both hands down his face.

He was *not,* he refused to be, in love with Deedee.

Why? a niggling little voice asked him.

Because loving someone was too risky. It set a guy up to be cut off at the knees, to be totally vulnerable to heartache and pain. Too risky.

Oh? Wasn't being a cop risky?

Ryan sighed in frustrated defeat.

Yeah, being a cop was physically and emotionally risky. And he was itching to get back into that uniform, to be what he was meant to be. He was once again prepared to run all the risks that being a police officer entailed.

To use "too risky" as a reason not to love was lame, didn't cut it. The risk of loving was no greater in his mind than the risks of being a cop. No, it wasn't the risk of loving that was causing a knot to twist in his gut.

It was . . .

Sherry.

Ryan swore and threw back the blankets. He sat up on the edge of the bed, rested his elbows on his knees and cupped his head in his hands.

The darkness in the room was oppressive, seeming to crush him with the weight of unwanted memories.

Sherry.

Since her death, he'd stood firm in his inner pledge to stay true to her, to honor the vows they'd taken until he drew his last breath.

He had told himself that what he'd had with Sherry had been fantastic beyond measure, was a once-in-a-lifetime experience that would make anything else second-best. They'd been so happy together, so connected. They'd had it all.

A chill swept through Ryan, and he straightened, bracing his hands on his knees as he stared into the darkness. The chill was followed by sweat that dotted his brow and trickled down his chest.

It's truth time, MacAllister, the little voice insisted.

The truth, his mind hammered. The truth. Oh, God, he'd buried it so deeply within him, couldn't face it along with the violence of Sherry's death. He'd left it there, the truth, hidden beneath his anguish, refusing to allow it to surface.

But now?

There was nowhere to run, nowhere to hide from the truth.

"Oh, Sherry," Ryan said aloud, his voice raspy with emotion.

They hadn't been happy together.

Her requested transfer to the emergency room had come through a few weeks after they'd been married, and everything had fallen apart before they'd hardly begun.

They rarely saw each other, and argued more often than not when they managed to spend time together. Sherry had refused to give up her coveted position. The more stubborn she got, the more demanding he became, telling her she *had* to leave the emergency room for a place with hours that matched his schedule more closely.

The last time he'd seen her before she was killed, they'd argued bitterly about the subject. He'd slammed out the door in a rage.

And he hadn't even kissed her goodbye.

Their marriage had been as good as over. Finished. They weren't going to make it together, and deep in his gut he'd known that, then buried the knowledge when she died.

There it was—the truth.

Ryan sat statue still, waiting for the pain to assault him, to rip him to emotional shreds. But instead, a strange sense of peace began to fill him with its warmth, moving slowly through him with a gentle, healing touch.

The heavy darkness in the room seemed suddenly lighter, brighter, allowing him to clearly see images flitting before him.

Deedee.
Dancing with the butterflies.
Deedee.
And he loved her.

Ryan sank back against the pillow, so exhausted he hardly had the strength to lift his legs onto the bed. He took a deep breath and let it out slowly, a groan of fatigue escaping from his lips.

Sleep, blessed sleep, began to creep over him like a comforting blanket.

He was in love with Deedee Hamilton, he thought hazily. He really, truly was. She was there, so clearly in his mind's eye, smiling at him, her dark eyes sparkling. Yeah, there was her cute nose with the adorable freckles, and her lips that were like sweet nectar.

Oh, man, how he loved her.

Ryan drifted off to sleep, not realizing that he was smiling.

The next afternoon, Deedee gave up her attempt to concentrate on the magazine she held. She set it back on the end table and shifted yet again in the less-than-comfortable chair.

She stared at the clock on the wall, willing the hands to move faster.

Ten more minutes. They'd said it would take an hour, and there were still ten long, agonizing minutes left to endure.

Then they would tell her.

Then she would know if she was pregnant.

She sighed wearily and leaned her head against the wall, closing her eyes. Images of Ryan immediately formed in crystal clarity in her mental vision—magnificent Ryan MacAllister.

The past weeks had been so fantastic. Little by little Ryan had lowered his guard, removed the walls around him to reveal, like slowly opening a tantalizing Christmas present, the wonder of the man he truly was.

He had a dry, witty sense of humor that had caught her off guard more than once, causing her to dissolve in laughter.

He listened, *really listened,* when she talked, as though everything she said was of the utmost importance to him.

She'd answered his endless questions about the running of Books and Books, and how she went about dealing in the rare editions, which were her pride and joy. He wanted to understand the inner workings of her business, he'd said, because it was a part of who she was.

Never before in her life had she felt so special, so cherished, by doing nothing more than being herself—open, honest and real.

And the lovemaking they'd shared! It was beyond description in its splendor. So beautiful, intimate... and theirs.

Ryan.

Whenever he appeared, her heart beat with a wild tempo and a smile instantly formed on her lips. The mere sight of him caused her to feel young, happy and vibrantly alive. She continually rejoiced in his very existence, and the fact that he was an intricate part of her life.

And she loved him with every breath in her body.

Deedee opened her eyes and stared into space.

She didn't know exactly when she'd fallen in love with Ryan, and had a sneaky suspicion she'd subconsciously ignored the reality for as long as she could. She'd broken the rules of their relationship, crossed over the boundaries they had set.

Friends and lovers.

Oh, yes, Ryan was her best friend. Ryan was her lover. But Ryan was also the man she loved.

And now she was waiting to learn if she was going to have his baby.

When she gummed up the program, she thought dryly, she didn't mess around. What if she really was pregnant? How did she feel about it?

She didn't even know, because she'd refused to address a maybe, an unknown. She was in limbo, on mental and emotional hold, waiting for that damnable clock to tick off the time until the unknown would become a known.

"Miss Hamilton?"

Deedee jerked in her chair. "Yes?"

"Dr. Mercer will see you now. You can go to his office at the end of the hall."

Deedee got to her feet, praying her trembling legs would carry her down the hallway.

"Come in, come in, Deedee," Dr. Mercer said when she entered the office. "Close the door and have a seat."

She did as instructed, gratefully sinking onto a chair opposite the doctor's desk.

Dr. Mercer looked, she'd decided years before, like Santa Claus out of uniform. He was a roly-poly man, with bushy white hair, a trim beard and the kindest eyes she'd ever seen. She liked and trusted him, but at that moment she wished she were a hundred miles away from him.

"Well, Deedee, we ran the blood test," Dr. Mercer said. "My dear, you are, indeed, pregnant."

Deedee blinked, opened her mouth to speak, then realized she had no air in her lungs because she'd been holding her breath. She gulped in some air and tried again.

"But I'm on the pill," she said, her voice sounding strange to her own ears.

Dr. Mercer shook his head. "I know, but your body has had a mind of its own ever since I've been your physician. You recall how many different varieties of the pill we had to try before finding one that would regulate you properly."

"Yes, but—"

"Your system simply overrode your method of birth control. It happens. I have a four-year-old-grandson who is proof of that fact. You *are* pregnant, Deedee."

"Well, fancy that," she said, attempting a smile that failed to materialize. "My, my, isn't that something?

If Forrest knew, he'd be putting The Baby Bet into operation. Forrest is Jillian's husband. They're expecting triplets. Can you imagine having three baby girls at once? They're all girls. Forrest won The Baby Bet about the triplets, but then he always wins The Baby Bet, you see. Everyone puts twenty dollars in the pot and—''

"Deedee," the doctor interrupted, a gentle tone to his voice, "hush."

"Oh, dear heaven," she said, then burst into tears. "I'm...I'm going...to have...a pink rabbit."

Dr. Mercer chuckled and pushed the tissue box on his desk toward her.

"It might be a blue rabbit, you know," he said. "Blow your nose."

Deedee nodded as she dabbed at her nose with a tissue. She took a steadying breath and lifted her chin.

"So!" she said, then threw up her hands, unable to think of another thing to say.

"All right, young lady," Dr. Mercer said. "You've babbled, then cried, which are par for the course. Now let's get serious. What about the father of your baby?"

"I love him."

"That's helpful."

"No, it's not, because he doesn't love me. We agreed to be friends and lovers, nothing more."

"I see. Well, perhaps this baby will change his mind about that agreement."

"No. No, nothing will. He isn't going to want any part of being a father, of having a more serious relationship."

"He played a definite part in your becoming an expectant mother." Dr. Mercer paused. "Deedee, do you want this baby?"

"Oh, yes," she said, a genuine smile lighting up her face. "I refused to get in touch with myself about how I felt about it until I knew for certain if I was pregnant. But I don't need even one second to ponder the question. I want this baby very, very much."

"You'll be a wonderful mother."

"*Single* mother."

"Perhaps. You do plan to tell the father about the baby, don't you?"

"Yes. Ryan and I are based on honesty. I'll tell him, but I'll make it clear that I don't expect anything from him. It's not his fault I have a weird system in my body. I assured him that I was protected. He's free of obligation here."

"That's all very noble, but what about the fact that you're in love with him?"

"*That* I won't tell him, because it wouldn't serve any purpose. It's not lying exactly, it's just leaving out a detail."

Dr. Mercer frowned at her. "Mmm."

"Trust me, I know what I'm doing." She got to her feet. "Thank you for being so kind, so caring."

The doctor stood. "Make an appointment at the front desk for about two weeks from now. Ask

MaryAnn to give you the packet of information for mothers-to-be."

"Yes, all right."

"Deedee, if you want to talk, I'm here to listen."

"Thank you, I appreciate that, but I'm fine . . . emotionally. I don't feel too swift in the mornings, though."

"Keep soda crackers by your bed and have a couple before you get up. The morning sickness hopefully won't last too long. We'll see how you're doing with that when you come in again."

Deedee reached across the desk and shook the doctor's hand. He smiled at her warmly, then she turned and left the office.

"If that Ryan fellow isn't in love with that sweet little girl," the doctor said to no one, "then he's seven kinds of a fool."

Chapter Twelve

Deedee vaguely remembered driving to Books and Books, thanking her employee for covering for her while she was gone, then assisting a customer who wanted a copy of *The Velveteen Rabbit*.

At last alone in the store, she slid onto the stool behind the counter, propped her elbows on the top of the counter and rested her chin on folded hands.

She was in love with Ryan MacAllister, her mind hammered. While sitting in the doctor's office, which certainly wasn't a very romantic place for such a discovery, she'd come face-to-face with the realization that she loved Ryan.

And if that wasn't enough to send her into a tizzy, she'd been told minutes later that she was pregnant with Ryan's baby!

It was too much to deal with all at once, just too, too much. Her mind was mush, and her emotions were a tangled maze.

She didn't know whether to shout with joy, or weep in despair.

"Calm down, Deedee," she told herself. "Take it one step at a time."

The bad news was that she was in love with a man who didn't love her in return.

The good news was that she was going to have a pink rabbit...or maybe a blue rabbit. There was no reason to have an ultrasound to find out if it was a girl or a boy. She'd simply wait for Forrest to announce that The Baby Bet was being held on her behalf, then listen for where he placed his money.

The bad news was that once she told Ryan she was pregnant, their relationship would be over. There would be no more lovely evenings together, no more exquisitely beautiful lovemaking. Ryan would be so angry that she'd moved beyond the boundaries of their being just friends and lovers.

Oh, dear heaven, how she would miss him.

The good news was that she was going to be a mother, would have a precious miracle, a tiny baby, to love and nurture.

Deedee sighed.

The good with the bad. The bad with the good. That's how it was, the bottom line. She'd learn to live with that. Somehow.

She straightened and placed her hands on her flat stomach.

"We'll be fine, little rabbit," she whispered. "We'll be a team, just the two of us, together."

My goodness, she was tired, felt emotionally and physically drained. She wanted nothing more than to go home, crawl into bed and sleep.

She glanced at the clock.

Forget *that* wish. She was working until she closed the store at eight o'clock. Ryan had telephoned that morning and said he had something important to share with her. They'd agreed he'd come to Books and Books at cight, they'd buy a pizza and go to her apartment.

Had that call from Ryan been just hours earlier? It seemed like an eternity since they'd made those plans, because so much had happened between then and now.

He had something important to share with her? Boy, oh, boy, did *she* have something to share with *him*. The sad part was that her "something" would cause him to walk out of her life.

Deedee sniffled and fought against threatening tears.

Get a grip, Deedee Hamilton, she ordered herself. She'd read the material she got at the doctor's office to find out the do's and don'ts for a mother to be. She'd concentrate on her pink rabbit, be happy, feel blessed. She'd stay in an upbeat mood if it killed her.

Until Ryan got there.

Until it was time to say goodbye to the magnificent man she loved.

She took a wobbly breath, then produced a bright smile as a customer entered the store.

It had been a long day, Ryan thought as he parked in front of Books and Books.

He turned off the ignition, but didn't move to leave the Jeep. He was twenty minutes early for his eight o'clock arrival, but had been unable to sit in his apartment a moment longer.

He was in love with Deedee Hamilton, he thought incredulously. He'd actually fallen head over heels in love. He was, to quote Ted, "down for the count." Even more amazing was the realization that he was *ecstatic* about that fact.

The ghosts of truth from the past had been dealt with, brought to the surface from the place within him where he'd buried them so deeply, then been flung far away from his reality of now.

He felt as though a crushing weight had been lifted from his shoulders. No, more than that. It had been removed from his mind, heart, his very soul.

He was free to live.

He was free to love.

And he loved Deedee.

Ryan frowned as he stared at the front of Books and Books.

He'd better come down off his euphoric high and address the issue that would determine his future happiness: *Was Deedee in love with him?*

According to Ted, Deedee was "down for the count," just as Ryan was. Having dismissed Ted as a blithering idiot at the time, he now wished to believe that Ted was right on the money, knew exactly what he was talking about. Ryan was in love with Deedee, and Deedee was in love with Ryan, so said Mr. Sharpe.

He'd buy Ted a dozen of Rosie's cherry pies if his partner had called it the way it was.

"Hi, Deedee," Ryan said to the steering wheel. "I'm rejoining the police force. Oh, and by the way, I'm in love with you. How do you like them apples, kiddo? Want to get married?"

Ryan groaned and rolled his eyes heavenward, then shook his head in self-disgust.

He was a wreck. There had just been too many hours to deal with while waiting to come to Deedee's store. He'd worked himself into a stressed-out, wired, tense mess. Talk about vulnerable. He was about to bare his soul to the woman who held his tomorrows in her hand.

Was Deedee in love with him?

Would she agree to marry him?

How would she feel about being the wife of a cop?

He had a choice. He could drive away from there right now, not run the risk of seeking the answers to his questions. Or he could go after the future he wanted with Deedee, risks and all.

"Go for it, MacAllister," he said, unsnapping the seat belt.

Deedee drew a sharp breath as she saw Ryan get out of the Jeep and start toward the door of Books and Books. She'd been aware of the exact moment he'd pulled into the parking place, and he'd jangled her nerves even worse than they were by sitting out there like a lump.

But now he was crossing the sidewalk to the door, turning the knob, pushing the door open and...

Oh, dear heaven, there he was. Ryan, the man she loved so very, very much. The man who was the father of the baby nestled within her. Her heart was thudding wildly, and an achy sensation in her throat was a warning that tears were once again threatening.

She would *not* cry.

They'd leave the store as quickly as possible, buy a pizza and go to her apartment. There, with class and dignity, being calm, cool and collected, she'd tell Ryan that she was pregnant and was assuming the responsibility for that fact.

Then she'd watch him walk out of her life forever.

Oh, Ryan.

"Hello," she said, managing a small smile.

Ryan didn't move from where he stood just inside the door. He stared at Deedee intently, a slight frown on his face.

He was looking at the woman he loved, he thought. He could hardly believe that this had happened to him. He was, by damn, in love. And, oh, man, it felt great.

He crossed the room, framed Deedee's face in his hands and kissed her, mentally cursing the counter that separated them.

The kiss was soft, gentle, reverent. The kiss was, to him, symbolic, an affirmation of his love for Deedee, a commitment to her and that love, a willingness to risk all and everything. The kiss caused his heart to thunder and emotions to momentarily close his throat.

He released her slowly, looking directly into her brown eyes as he straightened his stance.

"Hello, Deedee," he said, his voice raspy.

She tore her gaze from his, telling herself once again that she would *not* cry.

"How...how was your day?" she said, fiddling with the business cards in the plastic holder on the counter.

Fifty years long, he thought dryly.

"Okay," he said. He glanced at the clock. "We'll close the store in ten minutes and be out of here. We could call ahead to Mario's and order the pizza. Then it will be ready to pick up when we get there."

"I've got to finish unpacking a shipment first and marking the books off on the invoice. There should be several special orders in there that people are eager to have. I really need to have them available first thing in the morning."

"I'll do it. I've done it before without screwing it up. Should I put the books on the counter in the storeroom again?"

"Yes, thank you. All right, you go ahead and do that, and I'll start closing out the cash register, drop the shades and ... Yes, that's a good plan."

"Are you upset about something?" he said. "You're awfully pale and seem...I don't know...sort of tense."

"No, no, I'm fine. I'm just tired at the end of a busy day. And I'm hungry. Once I have some pizza and put my feet up, I'll be dandy.'' She smiled at him. ''Really, I will. Now shoo, you have a rendezvous with a half-emptied box in the storeroom.''

''Yes, ma'am,'' he said, matching her smile as he executed a crisp salute. ''Anything you say, ma'am.''

Deedee watched him disappear around the corner.

Anything you say, ma'am, her mind echoed. *I say I love you, Ryan MacAllister. Oh, God, how I love you.*

She shook her head and forced herself to concentrate on entering the figures from the cash register in a ledger book. A few minutes later she dropped the shade behind the front window.

Just as she reached to snap the lock in place on the door, it opened and two men entered, nearly knocking her backward.

''Oh,'' she gasped. ''You startled me. I was just locking up.''

''Do it,'' one of the men said gruffly.

''Pardon me?''

''Lock the door, lady,'' the other man said. ''We have private business to conduct here.''

''I don't understand what—'' she began.

One of the men pushed her aside, locked the door and dropped the shade on it.

''You've got some nice rare books we intend to take off your hands,'' he said.

''No!'' Deedee yelled.

Ryan stiffened, every muscle in his body tensing to the point of near pain. He'd heard Deedee's shout of

"No," heard the anger laced with panic. She was in some kind of trouble out there. She needed him. *Now.*

He started toward the half-opened door of the storeroom, then stopped, suddenly feeling weak in the knees as though he'd suffered a punishing blow to his solar plexus. Voices slammed against his brain.

Four-seventeen...shooting in progress...Sherry...shot...dead...Sherry is dead...four-seventeen...Deedee...Deedee is dead...dead...Deedee!...Deedee!...

Ryan shook his head sharply, then dragged trembling hands down his face.

Easy, MacAllister, he ordered himself. Calm down. That was then, before, old news. This was now, and Deedee needed him. The woman he loved was in some kind of danger. This was part of the risk of loving. Okay. It was okay.

Nothing was going to happen to his Deedee.

"Let's hurry it up, lady," one of the men said to Deedee. He took a gun from the pocket of his jacket and pointed it at her. He grabbed her arm, pulled her across the room and behind the counter. "Unlock that cabinet."

No! Deedee mentally hollered. Dear heaven, no, this wasn't happening. It was a nightmare, she'd wake up and... The silent alarm... The alarm. Oh, damn it, she hadn't activated it for the night yet. It was worthless the way it was.

Ryan. Oh, God, where was Ryan? The man had a gun. If Ryan heard what was going on, he'd come barreling out there and... No, please, no. He had to stay in the storeroom where he'd be safe from that hideous gun.

"Yes, I'll open it," she said, her voice quivering. "I'll do whatever you say. The keys are in the cash register under the change drawer."

"You're being smart, lady," the man with the gun said. "Just do as you're told and you won't get hurt." He released her arm. "Get the key."

Ryan inched his way along the wall, stopping at the corner. He peered carefully around the edge, his jaw tightening as he saw the gun in one of the men's hands. He ducked back, flattening himself against the bookcase behind him.

There were two of them. One was armed, the other might be. Ten bucks said these were the Culture Creeps Ted had been after for so long. They wanted Deedee's rare books, not the money in the cash register.

Had Deedee set the silent alarm? Probably not. She'd told him she'd gotten into the routine of turning it on just before she left the store, had made a pattern of her closing chores so she wouldn't forget to activate the alarm. No, there was no help coming from the police.

It was up to him. Deedee was his to love and his to protect. So be it. He'd get her safely out of this mess. He had to.

Ryan looked quickly around for something, anything, he could use as a weapon. He heard the ding of the cash register being opened and envisioned Deedee reaching for the key beneath the change tray.

The man with the gun was sideways to him, halfway blocking Deedee from view. The other creep was standing in front of the counter.

If he could take out the man in front of the counter, it would momentarily distract the one with the gun. He'd have to move fast, put all of his physical skills into maximum play.

He could do it. He *would* do it. Because nothing was going to happen to his Deedee.

He carefully lifted a thick, heavy book from the top shelf behind him, then peered around the corner again. Deedee was inserting the key in the lock on the cabinet. Turning the key. Removing it. Reaching up for the handle. Was wrapping her fingers around it and...

Now!

Ryan threw the heavy book like a guided missile toward the man on the outside of the counter. It caught him square in the head and he fell like a stone to the floor.

"What..." the other man said, spinning toward his partner.

At that moment, Deedee whipped open the cabinet door, smashing it against the man's head. He dropped the gun with a moan and instinctively grabbed his head with his hands. Ryan sprang forward and wrapped both arms around the man, flinging him facedown onto the floor, then dropped to one knee, which he planted firmly on the man's back.

"Call the police, Deedee," Ryan said.

"What?"

"The phone," he yelled. "Call the cops."

She did as instructed, her hands shaking so badly she could hardly press the three numbers for emergency service. As she gave the address of the store to the person who answered, Ryan took a roll of strapping tape from behind the counter and bound the hands and feet of the man he held pinned to the floor.

"You son of a—" the man started.

Ryan slapped a piece of the tape across his mouth, then hurried to secure the wrists and ankles of the man who was still groaning on the floor on the other side of the counter.

Sirens could be heard in the far distance as Ryan bolted to his feet and rushed behind the counter, pulling Deedee into his arms.

"Are you all right?" he said. "Please, tell me you're all right. If anything had happened to you I... You were fantastic the way you decked that guy with the cabinet door. Oh, man, are you okay?"

"Yes. No," she said, clinging to him. "I was so scared. I thought it was a dream and I'd wake up, but it was real, and I was terrified, and—"

"Shh," he said, stroking her back. "It's all over. Take it easy."

"And I was so afraid for you," she rambled on as though he hadn't spoken. "He had a gun, and you didn't have a gun, and I didn't want you to come out here because you might be hurt, and I couldn't bear that. And my baby. Oh, dear God, I was so frightened that they would do something that would harm my baby."

Ryan tensed, then gripped her upper arms to move her away from him so he could see her face.

"Your baby?" he repeated, frowning. "What baby?" His eyes darted to her flat stomach, then back to her face. "You're pregnant?"

Before Deedee could reply, the sirens filled the air and flashing blue and white lights were visible beyond the shades.

"This is the police," a voice boomed over a megaphone. "Put your hands up and come out. You've got five seconds. Do it."

Ryan stared at Deedee for another long moment, then turned and strode to the door, unlocking and flinging it open. He stood in the doorway, arms held high.

"It's a done deal," he called. "I'm Ryan Mac-Allister, cop on leave, but back in uniform tomorrow. Ted Sharpe is my partner. I think we've got your Culture Creeps in here. Come collect the scum."

"Hey, MacAllister," one of the police officers yelled, "glad to hear you're back. Thought you'd practice before you suited up again, huh?"

The store was instantly swarming with police.

Deedee watched the bustle of activity with a rather detached lack of interest, as though she was there, but not really there.

Ryan was going to become a police officer again? she thought hazily. He'd be back in uniform tomorrow? He was going to be Ted's partner?

That was wonderful, it really was. It meant he'd truly reevaluated his life, sifted and sorted, and gotten in touch with himself. He was returning to where he belonged by rejoining the police force, was putting the past behind him and moving forward with his life.

If only, oh, if only his future included her as his wife. If only he was going to actually take part in the raising of their child. What a fortunate baby the little pink rabbit would be to have Ryan MacAllister as a father on a day-to-day basis.

But that wasn't going to happen because she'd broken the rules of their relationship. When she told Ryan she was pregnant, he would...

Deedee blinked and came back to reality from her foggy place.

When she told Ryan she was pregnant?

She *had* told him.

It was becoming clear to her now. She'd zonked that awful man right in the head with the cabinet door, which had been extremely resourceful of her.

But then she'd babbled on and on as a result of being so frightened. She'd lost it. She'd come apart at the seams, and clung to Ryan all the while she was rambling on like an idiot. In the midst of that uncontrollable chatter, she'd told him about the baby!

"Oh, dear heaven," she said, her hands flying to her pale cheeks.

She'd intended to sit him down in her apartment and quietly explain the situation, not babble the news flash in a fit of hysteria.

Oh, dear, what was Ryan thinking, feeling, about what she'd said?

"Are you all right, ma'am?" a police officer said.

"Me?" she said. "No. Well, yes, but . . . no."

"Mmm," he said, nodding. He turned and looked around for Ryan. "Hey, MacAllister, you'd better take your lady home before she fades out on us here. She can come down to the department anytime tomorrow and make a statement for the record."

Ryan maneuvered through the crowded store to reach Deedee, but didn't look directly at her.

"Yeah, okay," he said to the officer. "I need to lock this place and set the silent alarm. You guys ready to wrap up here?"

"Yeah, we're gone. Those two you nabbed are singing their little hearts out in the patrol car. They're the Culture Creeps, all right. The reason there wasn't any word on the streets is because they have the stuff stashed, hadn't tried to fence any of it yet. We've been after these scum for weeks. You and your lady make a great team."

"That's us," Ryan said, no hint of a smile on his face. "A great team, really in tune with each other."

"Yep," the officer said. "Okay, you guys, let's clear out of here so the hero and heroine can go home." He looked at Ryan again. "Glad you're coming back on the force, Ryan. Ted must be whooping with joy."

Ryan nodded and shook the man's hand.

A few minutes later, the store was emptied of police officers. A heavy silence fell.

"Ryan . . ." Deedee started.

"Do you have your keys? Let's lock the cabinet, set the alarm and get out of here."

"Yes, all right. I . . . I don't think I want any pizza, though. Do you?"

He crossed his arms over his chest and looked at her, a muscle jumping in his tightly clenched jaw.

"No, I don't want any pizza," he said, a steely edge to his voice.

Deedee shivered, the sound of his voice and the anger evident in his expressive eyes causing a chill to sweep through her.

"What I want," he said, "is to talk. I want the truth. Do you think you can handle that for a change, Deedee? Do you think you could actually manage to tell me the truth?"

Chapter Thirteen

Deedee did not even attempt to talk to Ryan during the drive to her apartment. Tension and anger seemed to emanate from him like rolling, crashing waves that slammed against her.

She leaned her head back on the top of the seat, trying desperately to put aside the lingering horror of what had taken place at Books and Books, and concentrate on what was yet to come during the confrontation with Ryan.

Her world was falling apart completely, she thought dismally. She'd hoped so much that she and Ryan would part gently, at least remain friends, although no longer lovers.

Once she'd explained that her pregnancy was indeed an accident, per se, and that she was assuming full responsibility for it, she prayed that Ryan would understand that it had not, in actuality, been her fault. There was no blame to be placed anywhere, nor would she look to him for financial support for the baby, or emotional involvement.

It was to have been a mature, quiet discussion, where facts were stated and accepted as they were.

But now?

Dear heaven, Ryan was furious. He was also no doubt terribly hurt. The stinging words he'd hurled at her regarding telling him the truth for a change indicated that he was convinced she'd lied to him about...

About what?

Deedee opened her eyes and lifted her head, frowning in confusion.

Now that she'd calmed down enough to really analyze Ryan's reaction to the slip of her blithering tongue about the baby, just what exactly had set him off? What on earth was she supposedly guilty of lying about?

Deedee slid a glance at Ryan, seeing his clenched jaw and the tight hold on the steering wheel that was causing his knuckles to turn white.

Her own anger began to bubble within her, growing stronger by the second.

If he used his tiny brain to think, he'd realize they hadn't been together long enough for her to have kept her pregnancy a deep, dark secret for weeks and weeks.

Was that it? Was he accusing her of a lie of omission? Did he believe she'd been aware of her condition and not told him for reasons known only to herself? Well, she would straighten him out on that data, by golly.

Ryan MacAllister could very well owe her an apology before the forthcoming discussion was over. She didn't appreciate being accused of not being truthful, thank you very much.

Deedee folded her arms over her breasts and executed a very unladylike snort of disgust.

Ryan shot a glare at her, then redirected his attention to the traffic.

Deedee narrowed her eyes and pursed her lips.

There was just no other explanation for Ryan's fury. He'd pronounced her guilty of withholding the news of her pregnancy from him before she'd even had a chance to speak, to explain.

The nerve of the man.

She could be just as angry and hurt about the manner in which she'd learned he intended to rejoin the police force. How long had he known that juicy little tidbit, but hadn't bothered to tell her? That was a major event in *his* life, which she had the right to be told.

Ryan MacAllister should look in the mirror to see who was actually guilty of a lie of omission.

When Ryan parked the Jeep, Deedee got out of the vehicle without waiting for him to come around to open her door as he preferred to do. She started off, and he fell in step beside her.

Great, she thought dryly. She didn't have her car. She often left it parked behind Books and Books overnight when she and Ryan had made plans to leave for an event from the store. They would sleep at her place, or his, and he'd drive her to work in the morning. Each had a supply of toilet articles and several changes of clothes at the other's apartment.

But the frame of mind they were now *both* in, could very well mean she'd have to call a taxi in the morning because Ryan would be long gone.

Yes, she should have driven her own car home.

She should have kept her mouth shut about the baby until they were alone.

She should never have fallen in love with Ryan MacAllister, because her heart was going to be smashed to smithereens.

When they entered Deedee's apartment, she turned on every lamp in the living room, waved Ryan toward the sofa, then sat down in a chair opposite.

He slouched onto the middle of the sofa and spread his arms along the top. The closed, unapproachable expression on his face that Deedee hadn't seen in weeks was firmly in place.

"So, Ryan," she said, lifting her chin, "you're rejoining the police force, going to be Ted's partner again. I think that's wonderful. However, I feel I should have heard an announcement of that magnitude directly from you, not while you were yelling it out the door at a bunch of other cops."

Ryan shook his head. "Nice try, Deedee, but it won't work, not this time. You're attempting to get the ball into your court, be the injured party here as far as not being told something of importance. No dice."

"Oh? You don't believe I had the right to know about your career change before the world did?"

"Indeed I do. If you'll recall, I phoned you this morning and said I had something to share with you. I intended to tell you tonight that I was returning to the force. Ted knew, but I specifically asked him not to inform Captain Bolstad, or anyone else, until I'd spoken with you. I told Ted you had the right to know first."

"Oh," she said in a small voice. "Well, um, I see."

"Do you?" He shifted to prop his elbows on his knees, lacing his fingers as he leaned toward her. "Do you see that I had every intention of being up front and *honest* about what I was planning? Do you?"

Deedee frowned. "What is this emphasis on honesty and truth about, Ryan? I didn't plan to tell you the way I did that I was pregnant. I was upset and words were tumbling out of my mouth beyond my control. I was going to tell you about the baby tonight."

"And then our relationship would be over," he said, his voice low and ringing with anger.

"Yes," she said with a sigh, "because you—"

Ryan lunged to his feet and Deedee stopped speaking. Her eyes widened, and she moved as far back in the chair as possible as he crossed the room toward her. He planted his hands on the arms of the chair, trapping her in place.

She looked up at him, and a shiver coursed through her as she saw the raging fury evident in the brown depths of his eyes.

"Our relationship would be over," he said, "because I'd have done my duty." A vein pulsed wildly in his temple. "Stud service."

"What?" she said, totally confused.

"Damn you, Deedee Hamilton!"

He jerked up from the chair and dragged both hands through his thick hair.

"I don't understand what—" she started.

"Knock it off," he yelled. "Oh, you're good, very good. You ought to go on the stage, considering what a terrific actress you are. Me? I should be shipped to the farm for being so damn gullible."

"What are you talking about?" she said, matching his volume.

"It was all there, right in front of me," he went on, beginning to pace the floor with heavy steps. "It goes all the way back to the night at Mario's, and Forrest's pink rabbits. I knew then—damn it, I knew—that you wanted a baby."

He stopped his trek in front of her and pinned her in place with his eyes.

"You set out to get pregnant, to get your *own* pink rabbit. *You used me, Deedee!* You used me to accomplish that goal."

The color drained from Deedee's face as she stared at him.

"Truth? Honesty?" he shouted. "From you? God, what a joke. You reevaluated your life, all right. Did it up royally. You wanted a baby, and I was putty in your hands. So damn eager to get into your bed, time after time. How did you keep from laughing right out loud at how easy I was to manipulate?''

Deedee attempted to speak, to deny Ryan's horrible accusations, but she was so stunned, shocked, by the hateful words he was hurling at her, she couldn't find the words.

"Risk. Run the risk," Ryan said, a bitter edge to his voice. "No way, I decided. Not a chance. But you got to me, little by little, kept chipping away at the walls I'd built to protect myself, until I had no defenses left against you.

"There you'd be, smiling, so glad to see me, smelling like flowers, reminding me of a delicate butterfly. There you'd be, with those cute freckles on your nose. There you'd be, welcoming me into your arms, your bed, your body. Stud Muffin MacAllister, that's me."

"Ryan, stop it," Deedee yelled, then tears filled her eyes.

"Whew. Forget the stage. Go directly to Hollywood, collect two hundred dollars on the way. You can even produce tears at will."

"Ryan..."

"No more. I don't want to hear anymore of your lies. Risks. Oh, I did the risk-taking trip in spades, to the max. Want to know something else, Deedee? I fell in love with you. Funny, huh? Isn't that rich?" He laughed, the sound a harsh, brittle noise. "I loved again. I lost again. Big time.

"But you? Oh, you won. You got exactly what you wanted. A baby. You *are* happy about your nifty pink rabbit, aren't you?"

"Yes, of course I am, but—"

"Yeah, of course you are," he said, his voice suddenly low and flat.

He stared up at the ceiling for a moment, then looked at Deedee again. Two tears slid down her cheeks as she saw the raw pain in his eyes and etched on his face.

"Ryan, please," she said, a sob nearly choking off her words, "let me explain."

"There's nothing you can say that I want to hear. What should I do now, Deedee? Thank you for making me have the guts to rejoin the police force, be willing to run that risk again?

"No, I doubt you give a damn what I do. Well, you can't take that away from me. I'm going to be a cop, dedicate myself to being a cop and focus only on that. *Nothing else.*"

Deedee got to her feet, praying her trembling legs would support her.

"Ryan, you've got to listen to me. *Please.* You're accusing me of such horrible things, and they're not true. *I love you.*"

Tears flowed unchecked down her cheeks and along her neck.

"I thought our relationship would be over, Ryan, when I told you I was pregnant, because I'd broken the rules, gone beyond the boundaries of what we agreed we would have together. Friends and lovers, that's all we were supposed to be, but *I fell in love with you.*"

"Yeah, right," he said. "You just don't quit, do you? You really expect me to believe that you're in love with me? Do you think I'm too dumb to not have come out of the ether yet? I believed you when you said you were on the pill, that you were protected. How many lies do you expect me to swallow?"

"Oh, but I—"

He sliced one hand through the air. "That's enough. I've had all I can take. I'll make arrangements through an attorney to provide you with money, child support, every month."

"No!"

"Oh, let it not be said that a MacAllister didn't provide for his kid. You'll get your money." He turned and started toward the door. "Stay away from me, Deedee, just stay the hell out of my way."

"Ryan, wait. Dear God, you're so wrong about everything."

He grabbed the doorknob, then looked at her over one shoulder.

"I'll get over you in time," he said quietly, a weary quality to his voice. "I'll forget what you looked like, just as I did with Sherry. I'll even—" his voice was suddenly choked with emotion "—even forget about the cute freckles on your nose."

He opened the door and left the apartment. The door slammed so hard behind him that Deedee flinched as though suffering from a physical blow.

"No," she whispered, sobbing uncontrollably. "Oh, Ryan, no, don't go. Listen to me. Please, please, Ryan. I love you so much."

But Ryan MacAllister was gone.

And Deedee Hamilton wept.

Chapter Fourteen

Ryan entered his apartment and removed the gun and holster he was wearing. He wandered toward the kitchen as he unbuttoned the uniform shirt, then decided he wasn't hungry and changed his course for the bedroom.

He and Ted had been late getting off their shift of duty, as they'd apprehended a drunk driver and had been caught up in the paperwork of booking the belligerent man into jail.

In the bedroom, Ryan sank onto the edge of the bed with a weary sigh, then removed his shoes. A few minutes later, he was naked beneath the cool sheets, telling himself that this time, *this time, by damn,* he would fall asleep immediately and not awaken for at least eight hours.

During the two weeks since he'd stormed out of Deedee's apartment, he'd been extremely busy. He'd intentionally kept himself on the run, not wanting to have any empty hours to dwell on Deedee and her deception.

He had completed the paperwork to sell Mac-Allister Security Systems to the two installers, and it was now a done deal. He'd accompanied them on several bid presentations, the only aspect of the business where they had no actual experience.

Having contacted all his suppliers to explain the change of ownership, the installers had been guaranteed the same lines of credit and payment schedules. The men had changed the company's name to Superior Security Systems, and Ryan was now totally out of the picture.

He spent hours at the police target range, sharpening his somewhat rusty marksmanship. He poured over the policy and procedures manuals he still had from his academy days.

Oh, yes, he'd kept very, very busy.

What he hadn't been prepared for was the nights—the long, dark, solitary hours of the night, which he now viewed as his enemy.

Ryan groaned, dragged both hands down his face, then dropped his arms heavily to the bed.

This night, he knew, was going to be no different from the others. That last scene in Deedee's apartment would play over and over in his mental vision, every detail sharp and clear. The memories haunted him, taunted him, caused him to toss and turn, and get only snatches of sleep.

What a fool he'd been, he thought, for the umpteenth time. What a gullible, naive, vulnerable fool. Deedee had played him like a master fiddler, pulling his strings, making him dance to her tune. She was now pregnant, just as she'd set out to be.

Deedee Hamilton was going to have his baby.

She would get her pink rabbit, or blue rabbit.

His son, or his daughter.

His.

No, he ordered himself, he couldn't, wouldn't, think about that baby. He'd wanted a child for as long as he could remember, but not one conceived in deception.

He had to somehow close off his emotions regarding that baby. It was Deedee's, not his, and he would have nothing to do with it beyond providing financial support.

"Ah, hell," he said.

How long would it take for the memories of Deedee to fade? How long was he to suffer the pain of knowing he'd loved and lost again?

He felt split in two, as though he was operating on separate planes. For one half of him being a cop, having Ted as his partner, was good, really great. He looked forward to going on duty, would have gladly done double shifts to keep him in the arena where he was contented and fulfilled.

Except for one strained episode when Ted had asked how Deedee was and Ryan had snapped that the topic of Deedee Hamilton was off-limits, he and Ted were performing as partners as though Ryan had never left the force.

The other half of him was empty, hollow, cold and suffering pain beyond measure. Ryan, the cop, was doing fine. Ryan, the man, was smashed to smithereens.

Fatigue finally dulled his mind and he drifted into a light slumber. Deedee's voice began to whisper in the darkness, growing steadily louder.

Ryan, please, let me explain. You've got to listen to me. You're accusing me of such horrible things, and they're not true. Not true. Not true. I love you. Dear God, you're wrong about everything. I love you. I love you. I love—

Ryan shot upward to a sitting position, his heart pounding, his body slick with sweat.

Lord, he thought, his hands trembling as he shoved them through his damp hair. That hadn't happened before. He'd never heard Deedee speaking to him as though she were actually there in the room, her voice choked with tears.

You're wrong about everything. I love you. I love you.

"No, damn it," he said, his words echoing loudly in the quiet room.

He hadn't listened to her lies, hadn't wanted to hear any more of them. He'd slammed out of her apartment, shutting the door on her and what they'd had together.

And he hadn't even kissed her goodbye.

Sherry? Deedee? God, the ghosts were doing double duty, tormenting him. He'd squared off against the truth of his failed relationship with Sherry, put it to rest. He'd faced the fact that he'd left Sherry in anger and had never seen her alive again.

And now?

History was beginning to repeat itself. He'd left Deedee in anger, too. But she was very much alive, was haunting him with her tear-filled voice, begging him to let her explain, pleading with him to listen to her.

Ryan flung the blankets away, left the bed and began to pace the floor.

Was that what it was going to take to gain inner peace? Was he going to have to listen to Deedee's story, pile more of her lies on the mountain of them that was crushing the very breath out of his body?

Hell, he didn't want any part of that scenario. But he was desperate, couldn't go on like this. He'd try anything to escape from Deedee's clutches.

Okay, okay, he told himself. He had to do it. He'd go to see Deedee, tell her he'd listen to her spiel. Was that too risky? No, it would be fine, because he'd be prepared for the lies. He knew the truth of her devious plan to use him for nothing more than a means to her end goal of having a baby.

He'd listen and that would end it forever, give him closure and inner peace.

"Yeah," he said, returning to the bed. "I'll see her one more time. One *last* time."

And no, by damn, he wouldn't kiss her goodbye!

* * *

The next evening, Deedee tugged a T-shirt over her head, smoothed it onto the waistband of her jeans, then reached for the comb on the edge of the bathroom sink. After flicking her curls into place, she frowned at her reflection in the mirror.

Not good, she mused. Not good at all. She looked like she felt—exhausted. She hadn't been sleeping well for the past two weeks, not since that final, horrible scene with Ryan. On top of that, each new day had brought a spell of morning sickness that rendered her drained.

Deedee sighed, left the bathroom and went into the kitchen in search of dinner.

She'd had an appointment that afternoon with Dr. Mercer, who had declared her to be healthy, albeit a tad underweight. He'd given her a prescription to subdue the morning sickness, told her to eat more and to get some sleep, for mercy's sake.

She was approximately six weeks' pregnant, she thought as she opened the refrigerator. Dr. Mercer had established that fact today. That meant she had conceived Ryan's child very early on during the exquisitely beautiful lovemaking they'd shared.

She removed a carton of milk and a covered dish of homemade stew from the refrigerator, then bumped the door closed with her hip. After pouring a glass of milk, she leaned her backside against the counter and stared into space while waiting for the stew to heat in the microwave.

What a strange thought it was to now realize that during all the outings with Ryan, the evenings spent in each other's company, the wondrous nights of making love, their child had already been nestled deep within her.

They had been together—mother, father and baby—without even knowing it. A family. Mama, Papa and a little pink rabbit.

The microwave dinged and Deedee jerked in surprise at the tinny noise. A few minutes later, she was seated at the table, determined to chew and swallow every morsel of the nutritious meal.

A family, her mind echoed. How glorious that would be. She loved Ryan MacAllister so much, could envision being his wife, greeting him at the door with a loving smile when he got off duty, their child held securely in her arms.

"Deedee, just shut up," she ordered aloud, "and eat your dinner."

She was *not* being kind to herself by indulging in such an impossible fantasy. She needed to stay anchored in reality, accept the situation as it truly was.

Marriage to Ryan was not in the offing. He was convinced she'd used him, betrayed him, lied to him from the very beginning of their relationship. She was a woman alone, who was going to be a single mother, and she'd be just fine, thank you very much.

"So there," she said. "Now eat."

After finishing the meal and cleaning the kitchen, she went into the living room and settled onto the sofa with a thick novel. A moment later, a sharp knock sounded at the door.

"Encyclopedia salesman," she muttered, getting to her feet.

She crossed the room and peered through the hole of the safety-device in the door, her heart instantly quickening.

Ryan, her mind hammered. Ryan MacAllister was standing on the other side of that door!

She reached to undo the security chain, then hesitated.

Why? Why was Ryan there? What did he want?

If he thought for one minute that he could march in there and execute a repeat performance of his horribly unjust list of accusations against her, he was very mistaken. Not in this lifetime, mister.

Ryan knocked again. Deedee quickly undid the chain, unsnapped the lock and opened the door. She lifted her chin and looked directly at him, striving for an aloof, rather disinterested expression.

"Yes?" she said coolly.

Oh, dear heaven, she wanted to fling herself into his arms, touch him, kiss him, feel the strength of his magnificent body, inhale the aroma that was uniquely his. She loved this man so very, *very* much.

"Hello, Deedee," Ryan said quietly, no readable expression on his face. Deedee looked so tired, had dark smudges beneath her beautiful eyes. He wanted to scoop her up, hold her tight, ask her how she was feeling, tell her everything was fine now because he was there to take care of her.

MacAllister, he ordered himself, *get it together.*

"May I come in?" he said.

"Why?" Deedee said, raising her chin another notch.

Ryan glanced quickly along the hallway, then looked at her again.

"I'd like to talk to you," he said, "and I'd prefer to do it privately."

"And briefly," she said, stepping back to allow him to enter. "Very briefly."

She closed and locked the door, moved around him and resumed her seat on the sofa. She crossed her legs, folded her arms over her breasts and nodded toward the chair opposite her.

"Sit," she said. "Or stand. Whatever. I don't care. What is it you want to talk to me about, Ryan?" *I love you, Ryan MacAllister, you stubborn, unbending specimen of a man.* "Hmm?"

Ryan sat down in the chair, leaned forward and rested his elbows on his knees, then clasped his hands tightly.

"I, um..." he started, then cleared his throat. "Look, I keep going over and over that last night we had together, what was said and, even more, what wasn't said. I can't seem to put it away, because there are pieces missing."

"Oh?"

"You kept saying I should listen to you, let you explain things. That's why I'm here now—to listen to your explanation."

"So you can accuse me of lying again? No thank you, Ryan. You had your chance to hear the truth of what actually happened. I begged you to allow me to tell you the facts as they were, and you refused.

"Now you've decided you'll listen to me to fill in the blanks of your mental puzzle so that you can put it all away?" Deedee narrowed her eyes. "MacAllister, you can go straight to hell."

Ryan opened his mouth, ready with an angry retort, then shook his head and leaned back. He drummed the fingers of one hand on the arm of the chair for a moment as he reined in his temper.

"All right," he said finally. "Then I'll fill in the blanks with the data I have. You used me, lied to me, wanted nothing more from me than being the other half of what it would take to achieve your goal of having a child."

"That's not true! I was on the pill. I told you that. You even saw the package on the bathroom sink."

"A sink that contains a handy drain those fancy little pills could be washed down."

"Oh, you're despicable, you really are. You listen to me, Ryan MacAllister, and hear every word. My body has a mind of its own that has always proven difficult to regulate. My system overrode the birth control pills, which was not all that surprising to my doctor.

"I did *not* intentionally get pregnant. I did *not* use you as stud service, as you've so eloquently put it. I was torn in two about the baby. Once I knew I was pregnant, I realized I had truly yearned for a child, just as you'd said. The realization that I was pregnant, carrying your baby, was glorious.''

She drew a trembling breath, struggling against threatening tears.

"But the other half of me?'' she went on. "I was devastated. I knew our relationship would be over because I'd broken the rules, through no fault of my own. I'd gone beyond the boundaries of being just friends and lovers. I was going to lose you, Ryan.''

A sob caught in her throat. "And I did. And I love you so much.''

She waved one hand sharply through the air.

"Go away,'' she said, dashing an errant tear from one cheek. "Leave me alone. I'd like to salvage at least a modicum of my dignity. Go, Ryan. *Now!*''

Ryan's heart thundered so violently he unconsciously splayed one hand on his chest for a moment as he stared at Deedee.

Dear Lord, he thought, she was telling the truth. He had listened, really *heard,* what she'd said, and she was telling the truth!

The woman he loved, loved him in kind. She hadn't lied to him, hadn't used and betrayed him. No! She'd simply loved him, honestly and openly, just as he'd loved her.

And they were going to have a baby, a miracle.

Ah, Deedee!

But, oh, dear God, what had he done? There were tears in her big brown eyes, such pain in her voice and etched on her delicate features. He'd hurt her so badly, caused her such anguish. How could he make it up to her? Would she ever forgive him? Was it too late for him to undo the damage? No!

"Deedee," he said, his voice raspy with emotion, "I don't know what to say to you."

"Then don't say anything. I asked you to leave, Ryan. Now I'm telling you in no uncertain terms. *Go.*"

"No, wait," he said, getting to his feet. "Please, Deedee, listen to me. I believe you, I truly do. I know you didn't lie to me, didn't use me just to father a child.

"I believe that you love me, and I know I love you, I swear I do. I'm asking you—hell, I'm begging you to forgive me for doubting you. I want to marry you, raise our child together. I want—"

"*You* want?" she interrupted. "What else is on your list of 'wants,' Ryan? Do you *want* me to push a magic button and erase all your horrible accusations from my memory? Do you *want* me to burst into song because I'm so thrilled that you've come to believe me, believe *in* me, after all?"

"Deedee . . ." Ryan started toward her.

She got to her feet and raised one hand, palm out, to stop him.

"No, don't come near me," she said, then wrapped her hands around her elbows in a protective gesture. "Don't come near *me* or *my* baby." Tears began to slip unnoticed down her pale cheeks. "You say you believe me . . . tonight. I fantasized about hearing those words, but now I realize I have to think beyond them. What about tomorrow, then the day after that? Would you mull it some more and decide that, no, by golly, you were right the first time? Decide I used you, lied, betrayed you?''

"No! Ah, Deedee, I'm so sorry for what I did, what I said. Won't you please listen to me?''

"Hear the echo, Ryan? Those were my words two weeks ago. I begged you to listen to me, to the truth, and you refused." A sob caught in her throat. "How can you possibly expect me to believe *you* now? I'd be waiting for you to change your mind about me again."

"I wouldn't, Deedee. I love you."

"No, I can't do this," she said, shaking her head. "I can't live that way...waiting, wondering. It's too risky, too cold, too empty. I'd rather be alone. I'm tired, Ryan, exhausted. Leave, just leave."

Ryan stared at her, aching to go to her, hold her, demand that she listen and believe in him. Their whole future was at stake, and it was being flung away like grains of sand blown into oblivion by a whipping wind.

Deedee *had* to forgive him. She *had* to see that they could have it all, together. She *had* to...

Easy, MacAllister, he thought suddenly. He needed to slow down, regroup. Deedee, his beautiful, fragile butterfly, was wounded, so hurt, by what he'd done. She needed time to learn to believe in him again. He couldn't snap his fingers and set things to rights.

Yes, she needed time, *but not time alone,* to dwell on what he'd done. He had to think of a way to convince her to forgive him, a way to stay near her, front-row center, where she would be unable to begin to forget he existed.

"I'll go," he said quietly, "but this isn't over, isn't finished."

"Yes, it is," she whispered, tears still streaming down her face. "Yes, it is."

He started toward the door, then turned abruptly and retraced his steps to stand directly in front of her. He gripped her shoulders, hauled her to him and gave her a fast, hard kiss. When he released her, he looked directly into her tear-filled eyes.

"That kiss was important, Deedee Hamilton. Yes, I'm leaving but, by damn, *I kissed you goodbye.* That means I'll be back. I'm not giving up on us, on what we can have together. I love you, intend to spend the rest of my life with you and a whole bunch of pink and blue rabbits."

"No," she said, closing her eyes and shaking her head. "No, it's too late for us. Too late. Goodbye, Ryan."

"Good *night,* Deedee."

He kissed her gently on the forehead, then left the apartment, closing the door behind him with a quiet click.

"Too late," Deedee said, sobbing as she covered her face with her hands.

Chapter Fifteen

"Hell, MacAllister," Ted said, "when it comes to screwing things up, you're in the major leagues, buddy."

"I don't need *you* to tell me that," Ryan said. "Believe me, I know it. Big time. What I'm asking for here is some help, some advice, Sharpe."

"Yeah, okay," Ted said. "Well, shut up and let me think."

The pair had just finished a shift of day duty and were still wearing their police uniforms. Because Ted's car was in the shop for routine servicing, Ryan had picked him up that morning. They'd agreed to go to Rosie's for chili after work.

Now sitting in the café with steaming bowls of the

delicious chili in front of them, they ate in silence. Ted was deep in thought. Ryan was a study in misery.

His appetite gone, Ryan pushed the half-empty bowl to one side, then stared into space. He slid an occasional glance at Ted, as though hoping to glimpse a light bulb suddenly appearing above his partner's head.

"Pie?" Ted finally asked Ryan.

"No."

"Rosie," Ted hollered, "two slices of cherry pie, please."

"I said I didn't want any."

"Well, *I* want two pieces," Ted said. He leaned back in the booth and crossed his arms over his chest. "Man, oh, man, you really blew it with Deedee."

"Would you cut it out?" Ryan said, glaring at him. "I admit I'm a jerk. Okay? I'm a jerk. Ted, I left Deedee's apartment four nights ago with every intention of formulating a plan to win her back. So far, I've come up with zip, absolutely nothing."

He smacked the table with the palm of one hand.

"Every day that goes by and I don't do something positive toward getting Deedee to forgive me is dangerous. Each day is twenty-four more hours she's had to work toward forgetting me, putting me in some dark, dusty corner of her mind."

Ted nodded. "Yep. You've definitely got to get a plan, buddy."

"For what?" a woman said, placing two plates containing huge slices of hot cherry pie on the table. She was short, plump, with gray hair twisted into a figure-eight at the back of her head, and a warm smile always at the ready. "What do my favorite boys need a plan for?"

"Ryan has major heart trouble, Rosie," Ted said. "He's in love, but he messed it up royally. The lady in question loves him, but she doesn't *like* him. Do you know what I mean? We don't have a clue as to how he can get her to forgive him and take him back."

"Ah, I see," Rosie said. "Eat your pie. Well, it's good to know you're in love again, Ryan. It's bad to know you have troubles with your lady. Does she have just cause to love but not like you?"

"Yeah," Ryan said with a sigh, "she sure does. I accused her of something rotten, wouldn't listen when she tried to tell me the true facts. Then later I listened and believed her, but now she's lost her trust in me, won't hear *me* when I speak."

"I don't blame her," Rosie said.

"Thanks a lot," Ryan said.

"You reap what you sow," she said.

"Amen," Ted said.

"So!" Rosie said. "You have to court her, be romantic, break down her defenses. If she really loves you, you have a chance. Maybe."

"Court her?" Ryan said, raising his eyebrows. "People don't do that sort of stuff anymore."

"*You* do, as of right now. What does she like? You know, what does she have a weakness for?"

Ryan sighed again. "Pink rabbits and butterflies."

"There's your answer," Rosie said, beaming. "Be innovative, exhibit some imagination. Eat your pie. This will require all the energy you can muster."

"Amen," Ted said.

"Shut up, Sharpe," Ryan said. "You're really getting on my nerves."

"Oh, yeah?" Ted said. "You'd better be nice to me, chum. You're going to need all the help you can get with this fiasco. Pink rabbits and butterflies? Geez, whatever happened to flowers and candy? Rosie, bring Ryan the bill. This dinner is on him."

"Would you look at that?" Ted said. "Amazing. Those little baby tennis shoes are no bigger than my thumb. Hey, they've got racing stripes on the sides, the whole bit. Isn't that something?"

Ryan peered at the tiny shoes. "Yeah, you're right. I wonder how they make something that small with details like that?"

"Beats me."

"Good evening, Officers," a matronly woman said. "My clerk informed me that you were in our department. How may I be of service? Did someone in higher management telephone for police assistance? *I* certainly didn't."

In unison, Ryan and Ted glanced down at their uniforms, as though surprised to see them on their bodies. With Rosie's help, they'd formulated the first action to be taken in Ryan's campaign to make amends with Deedee. The two men had left the café and headed for the nearest large department store.

"Oh, we're not cops," Ryan said. "I mean, we are, but we're not on duty. We just haven't taken the time to change clothes since getting off our shift because this is an emergency situation."

"I understand," the woman said, obviously not understanding at all. "You have an emergency that brings you to the baby department?"

"Well, yes," Ryan said. "We started out in the toy section, but they didn't have what I wanted. The lady there suggested we come over here."

"Oh," she said. "Just what is it that you're looking for, sir? I mean, Officer?"

"A small pink rabbit."

"Or a butterfly," Ted interjected.

"No, I think the rabbit would be the best move," Ryan said. "That's the issue at hand, after all. The whole disaster is over the pink rabbit, and how I screwed up so badly. It's really more symbolic than the butterfly at this point."

Ted nodded. "You're right. Okay, we want a little pink rabbit." He looked at the woman. "Do you have one?"

The woman backed up a step and eyed them warily. "Over there." She waved one hand in the air. "There's a display of soft, baby-safe stuffed toys. I'll... I'll leave you to browse. If you have any questions, feel free to ask the clerk on duty." She pressed one hand to her forehead. "I'm going home."

"Thanks," Ryan said as the woman hurried away. He looked at Ted. "What's her problem?"

"I don't know. Cops shake people up sometimes." He paused, then laughed. "Could be, buddy, that she's never had two big guys in uniform show up in her department before, asking for a little pink rabbit due to our being in emergency mode."

"True," Ryan said, grinning. His smile faded as he glanced around. "Look at all this stuff, Ted. Baby paraphernalia. It's really sinking in that I'm going to be a father. It's great, just so fantastic."

"You're going to be a dead man if you don't mend fences with Deedee, dude. Come on, let's check out those shelves over there."

"A baby," Ryan said, following Ted. "Man, oh, man, I'm going to have a baby!"

"A baby?" Andrea said, her eyes widening. "You're carrying Ryan's baby?"

Deedee nodded. "I asked you to come to the store because I don't dare cry here, Andrea. This is the fifth day since I sent Ryan away. I've told you the whole story, and there's no denying it's a terrible mess."

"No joke. Ryan wouldn't listen to you, then you wouldn't listen to him. There is some good old-fashioned listening called for here."

Deedee sighed. "I was so hurt and exhausted. Ryan had been so hateful, accused me of lying and... Then suddenly he said he *did* believe me. I just couldn't deal with it. If he changed his mind once, what's to say he wouldn't flip the coin over again? I couldn't live like that. No, it's finished, just isn't going to work be-tween Ryan and me." She sniffled. "Oh-h-h, I'm such a wreck."

"Now calm down," Andrea said. "I know my brother can be a giant-size dolt at times, Deedee, but believe me, if that man says he loves you, then Ryan MacAllister is definitely in love with you. And you're in love with him."

"Yes, but..." Deedee started, throwing up her hands.

"I'm so happy for you two. I *knew* something wonderful was happening way back at the twins' birthday party." Andrea laughed. "Forrest will be so tickled. He'll be able to put The Baby Bet into operation down the road."

"Andrea, would you quit being so cheerful? Ryan and I aren't even speaking to each other. I'm upset and confused. I'm miserable. Yes, I love him, but my faith and trust in him is shaken so badly. I just don't see a happy ending in the picture."

"Deedee, you're understandably not jumping with joy, but you've got to settle down and think things through. Ryan made a mistake, a *big* mistake. Are you going to compound it by refusing to accept his sincere apology to you for what he did?"

"Well!" Deedee said with an indignant sniff. "Now *I'm* the villain?"

"Oh, sweetie, there aren't good guys and bad guys in this scenario. There are human beings who are fallible." Andrea paused. "Do you remember that movie that came out years ago where the characters said that being in love meant you never had to say you were sorry?"

Deedee nodded.

"At the time, I thought that was so-o-o romantic. But now? I don't agree with it at all. To me, as John's wife, being in love means you *can* say you're sorry. You'll be heard, understood, forgiven, and whatever had caused the upset is put behind you so you can move forward. Think about it, Deedee. Please."

"Move forward," Deedee said quietly. "Let the past stay in the past."

"Yes."

Before Deedee could respond further, the door to Books and Books opened and a man in a khaki messenger's uniform entered, carrying a clipboard and a small package. The box was wrapped in paper with pretty butterflies in pastel shades.

"Ms. Deedee Hamilton?" the man said, glancing at Deedee, then Andrea.

"Yes, I'm Deedee Hamilton."

He put the box on the counter and extended the clipboard toward her.

"Sign on line six please, ma'am."

Deedee did as instructed, then tentatively reached for the pretty package as the messenger left the store.

"Butterflies," Deedee said. "Aren't they lovely? I adore butterflies."

"Someone obviously knows that," Andrea said. "Open it before I pop a seam, due to the fact that I'm basically nosy."

Deedee carefully removed the paper, took the lid off the box, then brushed aside the pale pink tissue inside.

"Oh," she gasped.

She lifted the treasure out of the box. It was a soft pink rabbit, approximately five inches high. It had a smile on its face and a carrot between its paws.

Andrea peered into the box. "No card."

"It's from Ryan," Deedee said, sudden tears filling her eyes. "I know it is."

"Ah," Andrea said, smiling and nodding. "The plot thickens. I'm off to collect Matt and Noel. I'm not needed here any longer with my pearls of womanly wisdom." She gave Deedee a quick hug. "Enjoy your present. *And remember to think.*"

"Yes. Yes, I will. Thank you so much, Andrea. You're a wonderful friend."

"'Bye for now."

Alone in the store, Deedee brushed the stuffed toy gently against her cheek, then cradled it in both hands as though it were made of the finest crystal.

"Oh, Ryan," she whispered.

The stuffed pink rabbit that was delivered to Deedee at the store the next day was twelve inches tall, wore a perky sunbonnet and held a tiny bouquet of silk flowers. The same butterfly wrapping paper covered the box.

Deedee burst into tears and had to tell the next four customers who entered Books and Books that she was suffering from an allergy attack.

The following day, the pink rabbit was three feet tall.

"Oh-h-h," Deedee wailed.

"No," Ted said. "No way. Not a chance. Mac-Allister, get out of my face."

"Ted," Ryan said, "you've got to do this for me. I'm fighting for my life here. I got Andrea to find out Deedee's work schedule. She's leaving the store at six o'clock tomorrow night. It's perfect."

"It's ridiculous."

"Name your price."

"I'm not doing it, MacAllister!"

"A cherry pie from Rosie's every week for the next year. Fifty-two of Rosie's cherry pies, Sharpe. Count them. *Fifty-two.*"

Ted rolled his eyes heavenward. "Sold. You sure know how to hit a man where he lives. But so help me, MacAllister, if one cop, even one, hears about this, I'll strangle you with my bare hands."

"My lips are sealed."

"Fifty-two of Rosie's cherry pies?"

"Yep."

"Damn."

At five minutes to six the next evening, Deedee picked up her purse, moved from behind the counter and said good-night to Christy, the young woman who had come on duty at Books and Books.

"Have a nice evening," Christy said. "I'll... Aaak!" she suddenly screamed. "Oh, my gosh!"

Deedee spun around to see what had caused Christy's startling outburst.

"Dear heaven," Deedee said, her eyes widening.

Standing before her was a pink rabbit more than six-feet tall!

It had a big smile, bright eyes with long eyelashes, floppy ears and a fluffy round tail.

The rabbit shuffled across the floor to where Deedee stood by the counter.

"Come with me," the rabbit whispered.

A woman entered the store and immediately stood statue still, her mouth open.

"I . . ." Deedee started, then had to take a breath of much-needed air. "You want me to go with you?"

The rabbit nodded.

"Deedee," Christy said, her voice trembling, "you can't go off with just any rabbit that happens to walk in the door. What if it's a sex maniac rabbit or something? Oh, Lord, I'm hysterical."

"Damn it, Deedee," the rabbit said. "It's me . . . Ted. Would you just come on?"

"Ted?" she repeated.

"Shh, not so loud. If anyone learns about this, I'll have to leave town. Are you coming?"

Oh, Ryan, Deedee thought, a soft smile forming on her lips. Her wonderful Ryan was behind this crazy stunt. Andrea was right. It was time to forgive, put the mistakes in the past and move forward.

It was time to love Ryan MacAllister with all she was, the very essence of herself—heart, mind, body and soul.

"Yes," she said, "I'll go with you."

Ted bent one furry pink arm, and Deedee slid her hand into the crook of his elbow. They went toward the door, Deedee smiling pleasantly at the woman who still stood with her mouth open like a goldfish.

"Good evening, ma'am," Deedee said. "Goodbye, Christy."

"'Bye," Christy said weakly.

"The feet on this thing are too big," Ted said, shuffling along.

Deedee swallowed a bubble of laughter, her heart nearly bursting with love for Ryan MacAllister.

Outside, people slowed their pace, staring at Deedee and her escort as the strange pair started down the sidewalk.

"I'm going to kill him," Ted muttered. "He caught me in a weak moment. Fifty-two pies doesn't cut it. One hundred and fifty-two isn't enough. It's settled. I'm going to kill him."

"Don't kill him, Ted," Deedee said, smiling. "I love him."

"Oh. Well, in that case, this might be worth it. No, forget it. He's dead." He paused. "Are you two going to live happily ever after with your little pink rabbit?"

"Yes. Oh, yes."

"Amen."

In the next block, Ted stopped in front of a restaurant and opened the door. To the ongoing stares of people passing by, he bowed and swept one arm through the air.

"After you," he said.

"Thank you."

They entered the restaurant and were immediately greeted by a man in a suit and tie. He gave no impression that having a woman accompanied by a human-size pink rabbit arrive in the establishment was anything out of the ordinary.

"Ah, good evening," the man said. "We've been expecting you. Madam, if you'll come with me please?"

"I'm outta here," Ted said.

"Ted." Deedee stood on tiptoe and kissed him on his furry nose. "Thank you."

"Be happy. You both deserve it. I'm gone."

The rabbit shuffled back out the door.

"Madam?" the man said.

Deedee followed him across the crowded room, ignoring the strange looks and whispered speculations of the patrons. The man opened a door on the back wall; Deedee moved ahead of him, then heard the door click closed behind her.

In the center of the small room was a table set for two, with candles burning in crystal holders and champagne chilling in a silver bucket.

And standing by the table, looking magnificent in a charcoal gray suit, was Ryan.

"Hello, Deedee," he said, no hint of a smile on his face. "You came."

"I came," she said softly.

"I love you."

"I know."

"Deedee, right now, standing here, I'm more terrified than I've been in my life, including times when I was scared spitless as a cop. This is it. Nothing, or forever."

"Ryan..."

"I sent the pink rabbits to tell you, to hopefully convince you, that I... Ah, damn, I'm so sorry for the pain I caused you. Deedee, please, *please*, forgive me. Give me, us, another chance. I don't want to lose you, our baby, the life we can have together. Will you forgive me?"

"Only if—" tears misted Deedee's eyes "—you forgive me. You wouldn't listen to me, but I'm just as guilty of not listening to you. I'm so sorry, Ryan. I love you. Oh, God, how I love you. We'll put our mistakes in the past, we truly will. The future is ours. Will you marry me, Ryan MacAllister?"

"Oh, yes. Come here, Deedee Hamilton," he said, opening his arms.

And she went.

With tears of happiness spilling down her flushed cheeks, she rushed into Ryan's embrace, holding him fast as he wrapped his arms around her.

"Ah, my Deedee," he said, his voice choked with emotion. "Deedee."

She tilted her head back to meet his gaze, and neither made any attempt to hide the tears glistening in their eyes.

Ryan lowered his head and kissed her, sealing their commitment to forever, putting the pain of mistakes securely away in the past and dreaming only of their future . . . together.

Slowly and reluctantly, Ryan raised his head.

"Would you like to order dinner now?" he said, his voice raspy with desire.

"No. No, my love, let's go home."

Ryan nodded, then encircled her shoulders with his arm. "Home. *Our* home. The three of us."

"Yes," Deedee said, smiling. "Mama, Papa and the little pink rabbit."

The wedding was held in Andrea and John's back-yard with the MacAllister family in attendance. Spring flowers were woven through a wicker archway where the bride and groom stood before the minister. Vows were exchanged and simple gold wedding bands slipped into place.

"You may kiss your bride," the minister finally said to Ryan.

Just as Ryan leaned toward Deedee, she gasped softly. They both straightened in surprise that was immediately followed by delight.

A delicate butterfly fluttered between them, as though giving its blessing to their union. It glided gracefully upward, hovered a moment, then flew toward the heavens.

"Oh, Ryan," Deedee said, awe and wonder in her voice, "it's as though the butterfly is dancing, just for us."

"Perfect," Ryan said, watching the beautiful butterfly disappear from view.

"Amen," Deedee said.

Then Ryan MacAllister smiled.

And Deedee MacAllister did, too.

* * * * *

For more on the wonderful MacAllister family and their friends, don't miss the next installment of THE BABY BET, coming to you this spring from Silhouette Special Edition!

COMING NEXT MONTH

#1015 SISTERS—Penny Richards
That Special Woman!
Cash Benedict's return meant seeing the woman he'd always wanted but felt he had no right to love. Skye Herder had never forgotten Cash, and now he was about to find out that Skye wasn't the only person he left behind all those years ago....

#1016 THE RANCHER AND HIS UNEXPECTED DAUGHTER—Sherryl Woods
And Baby Makes Three
Harlan Adams was used to getting his way, but feisty Janet Runningbear and her equally spunky daughter weren't making it easy for him. Janet sent Harlan's heart into a tailspin, until he was sure of only one thing—he wanted her as his wife!

#1017 BUCHANAN'S BABY—Pamela Toth
Buckles & Broncos
Not only had Donovan Buchanan been reunited with Bobbie McBride after five years, but he'd just discovered he was the father of her four-year-old daughter! Now that he'd found her, the handsome cowboy was determined to be the best father he could be—as well as future husband to his lost love.

#1018 FOR LOVE OF HER CHILD—Tracy Sinclair
Erica Barclay always put the needs of her son first. But when she fell for Michael Smith, she was torn between passion and her child. Could she still protect her son and listen to the needs of her own heart?

#1019 THE REFORMER—Diana Whitney
The Blackthorn Brotherhood
Strong, loving Letitia Cervantes was just the kind of woman Larkin McKay had been waiting for all his life. And when her son's rebellious spirit called out to the father in him, he wanted to bring them together into a ready-made family.

#1020 PLAYING DADDY—Lorraine Carroll
Cable McRay wasn't interested in taking on fatherhood and marriage. But Sara Nelson made those thoughts near impossible, and her son was proving irresistible—and Cable was soon playing daddy....

Take 4 bestselling love stories FREE

Plus get a FREE surprise gift!

Special Limited-time Offer

Mail to Silhouette Reader Service™

3010 Walden Avenue
P.O. Box 1867
Buffalo, N.Y. 14269-1867

YES! Please send me 4 free Silhouette Special Edition® novels and my free surprise gift. Then send me 6 brand-new novels every month, which I will receive months before they appear in bookstores. Bill me at the low price of $3.12 each plus 25¢ delivery and applicable sales tax, if any.* That's the complete price and a savings of over 10% off the cover prices—quite a bargain! I understand that accepting the books and gift places me under no obligation ever to buy any books. I can always return a shipment and cancel at any time. Even if I never buy another book from Silhouette, the 4 free books and the surprise gift are mine to keep forever.

235 BPA AW8Y

Name	(PLEASE PRINT)
Address	Apt. No.
City	State	Zip

This offer is limited to one order per household and not valid to present Silhouette Special Edition® subscribers. *Terms and prices are subject to change without notice. Sales tax applicable in N.Y.

USFED-995

©1990 Harlequin Enterprises Limited

As seen on TV!
Free Gift Offer

With a Free Gift proof-of-purchase from any Silhouette® book,
you can receive a beautiful cubic zirconia pendant.

This gorgeous marquise-shaped stone is a genuine cubic
zirconia—accented by an 18" gold tone necklace.

(Approximate retail value $19.95)

Send for yours today...
compliments of ▼ *Silhouette*®

To receive your free gift, a cubic zirconia pendant, send us one original proof-of-
purchase, photocopies not accepted, from the back of any Silhouette Romance™,
Silhouette Desire®, Silhouette Special Edition®, Silhouette Intimate Moments®
or Silhouette Shadows™ title available in February, March or April at your favorite
retail outlet, together with the Free Gift Certificate, plus a check or money order for
$1.75 U.S./$2.25 CAN. (do not send cash) to cover postage and handling, payable
to Silhouette Free Gift Offer. We will send you the specified gift. Allow 6 to 8 weeks for
delivery. Offer good until April 30, 1996 or while quantities last. Offer valid in the U.S. and
Canada only.

Free Gift Certificate

Name: _____

Address: _____

City: _____ State/Province: _____ Zip/Postal Code: _____

Mail this certificate, one proof-of-purchase and a check or money order for postage
and handling to: SILHOUETTE FREE GIFT OFFER 1996. In the U.S.: 3010 Walden
Avenue, P.O. Box 9057, Buffalo NY 14269-9057. In Canada: P.O. Box 622, Fort Erie,

---

FREE GIFT OFFER   079-KBZ-R

ONE PROOF-OF-PURCHASE

To collect your fabulous FREE GIFT, a cubic zirconia pendant, you must include this
original proof-of-purchase for each gift with the properly completed Free Gift Certificate.

079-KBZ-R

Silhouette

SPECIAL EDITION ™

AND BABY MAKES THREE

The Adams men of Texas
all find love—and fatherhood—in most unexpected ways!

The latest Silhouette Special Edition miniseries by

SHERRYL WOODS

concludes in March with

THE RANCHER AND HIS UNEXPECTED DAUGHTER
(Special Edition #1016)

Harlin Adams never thought he'd find true love again. But when a feisty younger woman and her rebellious daughter enter his life, bringing him lots of affection—and lots of trouble—he's willing to reconsider....

And if you missed the other books in the series—**A CHRISTMAS BLESSING, NATURAL BORN DADDY, THE COWBOY AND HIS BABY**—be sure to order your copies today!

---

if you missed either of the first three books in the AND BABY MAKES THREE series, A *Christmas Blessing* (SE #1001), *Natural Born Daddy* (SE #1007), or *The Cowboy and His Baby* (SE #1009), order your copy now by sending your name, address, zip or postal code along with a check or money order (please do not send cash) for $3.75 ($4.25 in Canada), plus 75¢ postage and handling ($1.00 in Canada), payable to Silhouette Books to:

In the U.S.	In Canada
Silhouette Books	Silhouette Books
3010 Walden Ave.	P.O. Box 636
P.O. Box 9077	Fort Erie, Ontario
Buffalo, NY 14269-9077	L2A 5X3

Please specify book title with your order.
Canadian residents add applicable federal and provincial taxes.

SWBAB4

You're About to Become a *Privileged Woman*

Reap the rewards of fabulous free gifts and benefits with proofs-of-purchase from Silhouette and Harlequin books

Pages & Privileges™

It's our way of thanking you for buying our books at your favorite retail stores.

PROOF OF PURCHASE
SSE-PP100

Offer expires October 31, 1996

**Harlequin and Silhouette—
the most privileged readers in the world!**

For more information about Harlequin and Silhouette's PAGES & PRIVILEGES program call the Pages & Privileges Benefits Desk: 1-503-794-2499

SSE-PP100